# Tales for Asti

# TALES FOR ASTI

## Twelve Stories to Read to Your Dog

*Isolde Kona-Dovale*

VORONA PRESS

*Abiquiu*

The stories in this book were greatly strengthened and expanded by the input and expertise of many friends, neighbors and colleagues. I would like to thank Dr. Eva Jablonka of The Cohn Institute for the History and Philosophy of Science and Ideas, Tel-Aviv University for her professional comments and insights; and thanks to my friends Natasha Makarova-Thaman and Vassily Lyashenko who helped me with all things Russian. I am deeply grateful to Hilda Joy for her careful copy-editing of the text. And to my special circle of friends, artists all — Dana, J, Suzanne and Gertraud — your enthusiasm for and support of this book was essential to its completion.

My husband gave me the freedom and space to follow my dreams, and encouraged me to create this book. Danke.

Julie Wagner created the beautiful woodcuts used in the text. JB Bryan oversaw the book's design and production with skill and gentle humor. And Lesley Poling-Kempes worked with me from the beginning of the project, and has patiently guided my on-going journey from a science writer to a creative writer. Many thanks to all of you!

*In memory of Asti and Lami*
*For Arnica*

You may send Isolde and Arnica a message at isolde@talesforasti.com, and visit their website talesforasti.com.

A portion of the proceeds from this book support the Española Valley Animal Shelter and Española Valley Humane Society. You can visit their website at evalleyshelter.org.

Printed in the United States

Vorona Press
P.O. Box 613
Abiquiu, New Mexico 87510

# CONTENTS

# Prologue

W hen it comes time to sit down and read a story to my dog, Asti, there are simply too few stories that we both enjoy. Because I am the reader, I am the one to choose the story. Although I turn again and again to those tales I like to hear, I have come to realize that Asti does not always share my enthusiasm for a particular story. She often falls asleep midway, or wanders off for a drink of water, or sits by the window and stares out at the birds on the patio.

I realized that we needed one book where all of Asti's favorite stories were gathered together. This book would be familiar in sight and scent to Asti, and she would know when I opened this book that each of the stories were for and about dogs. And I could read aloud to Asti knowing I was giving her world view equal time with mine.

So here is the book of Asti's most beloved dog stories. They are organized according to the month in which they occur or somehow belong. They can be read in any order, especially since the calendar year is a human invention that Asti and her canine friends have little use for.

All of the stories are about dogs, and are either narrated by a dog or told from a dog's point of view. They are from all over the world and are both contemporary and historic in place and theme. Although they contain many truths and insights into Asti's world, these stories are all fiction. Many of the dogs and their masters are based on real characters, and their stories are linked to actual events in the dog and human world. Several of the tales are myths. At the beginning of each tale, there are notes that give the human reader additional background about the story's origin. You may read them aloud or not. Asti feels the information is superfluous.

As you read these tales aloud to your dog, I recommend that you insert his or her name frequently into the text of each story. Asti likes this very much, as it places her into the story and brings the story into the present moment, which is the only moment a dog cares about anyway. Asti thinks story telling ought to be more of a conversation than a lecture. Also Asti tells me that dogs very much like to be involved in human conversation, even though they don't participate with words.

The dogs in these tales do use words, at least amongst themselves, which may be why Asti enjoys hearing them over and over again. I asked her just now if this is, indeed, the case, and she wagged her tail in what I understand to be the affirmative.

# JANUARY
## Siberian Feast

My doctor finally scheduled a series of barium tests. He, like me, was tired of listening to my endless and repetitive complaints of indigestion, heartburn, diarrhea, constipation, stomach cramps, and a half-dozen other minor but annoying internal disorders. While getting prepared for the procedure, I visualized the route the barium would take from the beginning to the end of my digestive tract. Not a nice picture. If God were an architect, he might have created a more scenic route from the upper to the lower body, rather than what I thought was a rather twisting, tedious and even disgusting track. I knew, however, that my dog had a different opinion of the whole apparatus and would appreciate every inch of it.

Although the story that follows is a favorite among dogs, especially Dachshunds, the human reader should be forewarned; part of this story takes place inside the digestive system of a hibernating bear.

*Omsk, Siberia 1917*

Tyapa the red Dachshund came home from a stroll through the small town of Omsk and found the door to her master's hut propped open. Before Tyapa even set a paw inside the hut, she knew that something was amiss. Her master would never leave the door open because the Siberian winters are very cold. Tyapa entered the dark hut and looked around; there was no fire and the samovar was not lit. Not good. Tyapa nudged the door closed and then crawled under a blanket in the corner. All Tyapa could do now was wait.

It had happened before. Tyapa had come home and found the hut cold and dark, her master nowhere to be found. Sometimes it was the vodka — a drink that was almost more plentiful in Siberia than water — that kept her master out all night. Tyapa herself could not tolerate even the smell of the clear liquid, but her master said it kept him warm and helped him to sleep. It also helped him to stumble, fall, grumble, curse, laugh, and be sick. Tyapa thought it was surely easier to just find a few scraps of wood, build a fire and curl up in a blanket. But master came home with vodka more often than with firewood.

If he came home at all. Once Tyapa's master was picked up and detained by men in uniforms who showed him a paper that claimed he, a peasant, had been conscripted to the White Army. Tyapa watched from the shadows as her master was taken away. He was gone for most of the spring. Another time her master was taken right out of their hut because he went to temple, not to church. After he returned from a few weeks in prison, Tyapa's master stopped going to temple altogether and started drinking the vodka instead. Then there was the morning Tyapa's master was taken from the hut by the other army, the Red Army. So many months passed, and Tyapa thought she'd never see her master again. And then he returned one winter night, thinner than before, but happy to be home.

Tyapa is a red Dachshund, and her master used to say red is the color of beauty. Now red is the color of one of the terrifying armies; red is also the color of the blood all of the armies cause to run in the Russian snow. So Tyapa knows that red is not beautiful to her master anymore.

Tyapa dug deeper into the blanket in the corner of the hut. She listened to the soothing sound of the railroad, the Trans-Siberian Railway, which passed by the hut several times every day. Even on a dark night, it was a happy, monotonous sound. To Tyapa it was almost like meditation. She grew up with this sound, and, even when Tyapa was a cold and hungry, the sound of that train put her to sleep.

A grumbling stomach wakens Tyapa at dawn. Although her master was very poor, he did manage to eat supper every evening. He was a good master and shared his meager table scraps with Tyapa. But master did not come home last night, and this morning Tyapa is frantic with hunger. Tyapa leaves the little nest she has made in the blanket and looks around the hut. Her master, wherever he is, must be as hungry as Tyapa this cold morning. Tyapa's hunger pushes her out the door of their little hut in search of her master.

Tyapa picks up her master's faint scent on the snow-packed road through the village and out along the railroad tracks. The scent leads to a railroad wagon. Fortunately, since Tyapa's master is very poor, and her diet consists of whatever her master can find to feed her, Tyapa is a trim Dachshund and can easily jump up and squeeze through the rotting wood slats of the wagon.

Inside the train wagon Tyapa, although happy to escape the cold Siberian air in a warm place, finds that her master's scent has suddenly faded. It has been replaced with a stench that would be nauseating for humans. Tyapa knows her master is not here and that she ought to turn around, go back out into the cold, and pick up his scent trail. But the stench that would drive away all humans is the most attractive, enticing aroma for a dog, and Tyapa remains in the train wagon. She follows the smell further into the wagon until she comes upon something large and hairy, wrinkly, bony, and warm.

Tyapa's mission to find her master is suddenly and happily derailed by what she finds in the wagon: a sleeping bear! Between two rows of very large teeth is the entrance to a very smelly and promising tunnel! Tyapa, being long and slender, crawls in, somersaults down a narrow hatch, and lands with a big splash in a dark cave filled with a vinegary, salty solution.

Tyapa is very still until she gets used to the dark of the wet cave. Her senses tell her that she is surrounded by soft stalagmites and stalactites. Tyapa dances about on this moist trampoline until she feels a prickling on her skin. The strong acid solution begins to burn her fur and Tyapa searches for a way out.

Deep down in a corner she finds a trap door. Being a Dachshund, Tyapa knows how to use her nose, mouth and paws to dig into a hole (she has practiced in her master's backyard). She quickly squeezes through the hole she has widened into a new place, a different environment. Where has she known these kinds of tassels before? Tyapa cannot remember. But it doesn't matter because she picks up a whiff of an altogether different and wonderful smell. Tyapa follows this wonderful scent into Dachshund-heaven!

Tyapa is surrounded by what humans call intestines, or chitterlings. She works her way through several delightful courses. Although this bear was neither a gourmet nor a gourmand, it is the finest feast Tyapa has ever known.

But even the hungry Tyapa can eat only so much. Suddenly she remembers why she is here! She must nose her way out and find her master.

Tyapa is happy that this old bear has not had food for some time because she can see the light at the end of the dark tunnel. Tyapa pushes her slender body down to the end and easily jumps out, shakes off everything not attached to her, and begins to pick up the scent she had followed into the train wagon. A slight but distinct scent pervaded the wagon even throughout the time she was within the bear. Could it be her master? Tyapa follows the familiar smell, and it leads her through a narrow opening into the adjoining wagon. And there he is, slumped over in the corner, snoring.

Tyapa leaps onto her master and kisses his face and hands. His breath, reeking of cheap vodka, is as potent as Tyapa's breath, reeking of bear innards. Tyapa's enthusiastic kissing, and the rancid quality of her breath, quickly wake up her master. He is delighted that his devoted Dachshund, Tyapa, has come to find him. As master embraces his smart, happy dog, all thoughts about war, bloodshed, prejudice, hunger, misery, even vodka vanish. And for Tyapa and her master the color red is once again beautiful.

# FEBRUARY
## The Birthday of Patience

WHAT HAPPENED TO THE DOG in this story happened to, I am sure, many dogs and people, including my dog and her master.

*Abiquiu, New Mexico*

February 6, 6 a.m. I can hardly wait until my master opens her eyes! At least *one* eye. Please! I know my master always waits to rise until the sun comes up over the rim of the mesa and performs her first daily task, which is to warm up the living room. I have fur so I am not cold, even before the sun rises. I watch my master sleep and think that surely we can get up early this morning. After all, this is a special morning. It is my birthday!

I know today is my birthday because I have been watching the moon. I have been counting the full moons as they come and go. I am three years old today. What a happy three years it has been, except for the time when I could not walk for a few weeks. I don't know what happened to me. One day I just woke up and had no feeling in my hind legs. It did not hurt, just no feeling. But I am a lucky dog. I had help from my loving master and all the humans in my small world, which actually is not so small because I have traveled to several continents and met many different people. Some of those people talked funny; they could not pronounce my name. I don't mind. I like people. However, once I overheard a person say that dogs have a lower IQ than people. Really? Then why can't they call me by my proper name?

Finally, master opens her eyes! Joy! I jump all over her and give her the usual good morning smack. She rubs my ears, neck, back, and many other parts of me I don't know the names for. She wishes me a happy birthday. I jump off the bed and wait while she rubs her feet. Then we go down to the bright, warm sun-filled living room. I make a quick trip to the cold outside to do my business, and then I am back in the house.

Master makes her usual breakfast. When she's done I get to lick the plate. And then it is time for my breakfast. But today I do not get my usual breakfast. I am given fresh liver. I try it. I am not so sure I like liver. The usual daily routine, already changed by that liver, is stopped altogether. My master is preparing a bath. For me! Some of my brothers and sisters may like to take baths, but I don't. I like to dive my head into muddy water. But a shower with smelly soap? No, that does not suit me at all. But it is my birthday, I am three years old, so I endure special things like a bath.

Even I must say that once my coat has dried and my body temperature has returned to normal — thank goodness for the warm sun! — the bath does not seem so bad. When I walk past the glass door and see myself, I am very pleased. My fur is shiny, black and tan. Yes, it is a good hair day just for my birthday. The soap odor will be masked as soon as the door is opened and I roll in the sand. Yes, there is a lot of good-smelling sand because we live in the high desert.

Now I am ready to receive my birthday guests. I sit at the front door looking out toward the driveway where my friends will come soon with birthday gifts. I hope for new toys because last year's toys have lost their voices and their innards. I am ready for new toys. I wait.

It is lunchtime and my master is fixing something awful smelling for herself. I am glad I don't have to eat lunch. I continue my patient waiting. My friends will come, I know. The sunbeams come in through all the windows to warm the house, all this for my birthday. My friends know my house will be warm and inviting. They know it is my birthday. They will come soon.

The sun has moved across the sky and now heads for the horizon, which is the top of the mesa to the west of the house. Doesn't this mean it is late afternoon and that darkness will set in soon? I know they will come. Patience. I listen for the click of the gate as it opens. But I do not hear it, nor do I hear the gravel of the driveway moan under the weight of an arriving car. They will come.

At least the moon does not let me down. The moon rises high in the sky above the mesas, surrounded by stars. So many stars! My friends know I have a birthday. There are three candles on the cake. Cake? Oh yes, my master baked a cake just for me, fortunately not with liver. I have made up my mind: I definitely do not like liver. Perhaps it is those chemicals that are supposedly good for me. Not everything that is good for us tastes good. The other organ I refuse when my master offers it is kidney. I like to smell kidney, but I will never eat it. And heart? I have not tried heart, but it must be good or there would not be so many songs written about the corazón (I learned this word from my Chihuahua friend, who ought to be here on my birthday).

The cake smells heavenly, whatever it is. I really would like to share it with my friends, so I wait.

My master has settled down to watch the PBS News Hour, BBC World News, then a Nature show about some animals, not dogs though. And then we watch the Jon Stewart Show, the Colbert Report, and the local news. How awful! Only robberies, shootings, fires, earthquakes, and floods. I want to hear what is going on in the dog world! Who won the Westminster Kennel Show? Who was that dog that pulled out skiers from under an avalanche in Switzerland? Who had the most puppies, loaned their ears to the deaf, and guided the blind across a busy street in Manhattan? What dog surrounded and held together a herd of sheep in Australia, saved his master from drowning, or kept a baby warm in a tent in Mongolia? Those are the stories I want to hear.

Oh no, Charlie Rose has come on TV. That means it is soon time to get ready for bed. Did I remember correctly? No one came to wish me a happy birthday. Maybe I have made a mistake, counted too many moons. Or not enough moons. Maybe tomorrow is my birthday. Lucky I saved my cake. I will share it with my friends when they come tomorrow.

# MARCH
## The History of 'Our Day'

As a child growing up in a small Bavarian town, I loved to fly my kite on the *Warenbichl*, the Trading Hill, a place name that recalls the town's ancient German-ic-Roman history. Beginning in 500 BC, the Romans constructed a road system which spanned more than 250,000 miles. Roads radiated from Rome in all directions, reaching as far south as North Africa and north into present day England. In 20 AD the Romans added a network of walls, called *limes*, which provided safe transport of goods and rapid communication of news throughout the Roman Empire. The *Warenbichl* in my home town was the station for the merchants along one section of the *limes* running from Rome across the Alps to the Rhine. On their way north, the merchants passed through Rottweil, a town founded by the Romans in what is now the south of Germany. The Rottweiler dog, supposedly a butcher's dog, was named after this town. Today there are only remnants left of the Roman *limes*.

*Rottweil, Germany*

Max, the leader of the Rottweiler pack, is well prepared for the arrival of spring. All year he has kept a close and careful watch over the number of full moons and made note of the coming and going of the seasons. He knows precisely when the day and night will be equal. Max knows it is time to notify all of the dogs in the little town of Rottweil of the annual celebration.

Just as he did last year, and every year for as long as the village dogs can remember, Max has secured a plentiful supply of bones for the upcoming Rottweil village feast, known locally as R-Day.

The village dogs have all successfully endured another long, cold winter in the mountain community. Max knows they all look forward to his announcement that spring has arrived and it is time for the annual 4 Bs: the bark, bite, binge and bash.

After making the rounds of the village and telling all of the dogs it is time to celebrate, Max returns to his home territory near the town square. Max laments the fact that several of his clan will not be at liberty to attend. This is because their masters, ignorant about their dog companion's annual feast, have planned their dog's day without consideration of the celebration. And as most dogs have a sense of responsibility and loyalty to their masters that does not permit disobedience, Max knows those dogs will go with their masters and miss the feast.

"How much better off the humans are," Max thinks as he watches the villagers and their faithful dog companions come and go in the square. The humans have special laws for their holidays; they do not have to go to work, can sleep late, eat whenever they want, take a nap, watch television, visit friends, and get paid as if they had worked for the whole day too. From all of his years of watching, Max has come to know a little about the world of humans. He suspects that most humans, although they celebrate holidays, do not care or even know exactly what those holidays are that they're celebrating. So of course the humans would not understand what the dogs were celebrating! But then, most of the dogs around Rottweil have no idea what they are celebrating on R-Day! Dogs and humans, Max knows, are not so very different.

The holiday arrives. There is still snow on the mountains, but down in the town it is a warm first day of spring. A great canine crowd gathers in Max's territory near the center of the village. On this one day only, Max permits the other dogs of the town to mark his territory near the square, and they all do so with great pleasure, lifting legs or squatting everywhere. A short barking concert follows, accompanied by the ringing of the bells in the church tower at noon.

After the annual lifting of legs in the town square, one young dog is selected to embark on the youth leadership trial. This young dog, chosen because of his strength, intelligence and nerve, is given instructions to roam around town and find a villager and bite him. Not too hard or deep. Just a small bite. If the young dog is not caught by the humans, he is eligible to join the elite group of village dogs from which the next leader (after Max departs, of course) will be selected. This year, as every year, the chosen juvenile leaves the square and goes out into the village with great expectations that he might one day be the leader of the pack, as big and powerful as old Max.

After the youngling has departed on his quest (which could take all day), Max reveals the many bones he has managed to save and bury over the past year. An audible wave of oh's and ah's is followed by a good half-hour of contented gnawing and chewing. By mid-afternoon all of the village dogs settle down in the spring sun for a good long nap. As is customary, Max will tell a story that is meant to put everyone to sleep. Max keeps his stories simple and to the point because he knows that his pack's attention span is very small and that their urge for an afternoon nap is very large.

Max takes his place near the fountain to begin his storytelling. He sits in silence for a few moments, deciding which of his many stories he will tell today. He has told the same stories over and over. Max is sixteen years old, and he knows he does not have many R-Days left. And there is still one story he has never told. Max has waited all these years for the right day to tell the Big Story — the history of his pack. How will he know when it is the right day? What if he misses the right day? Will any of the dogs be awake to listen? If not, the history Max carries in his memory will be lost forever. And Max will have failed as leader of the Rottweil pack.

Some of the dogs have already begun to doze. Resigned, Max begins to tell the well known story about the blind carpenter and his faithful dog: "Once upon a dog time..."

Max is hardly through the first sentence when he is interrupted by one of the little pups, a wide-eyed runt who has come to sit beside Max.

"But how did we get here?" the little pup asked Max. "Where did we come from?"

Several of the older dogs shushed the wee puppy and told him to lie down and go to sleep. The puppy, however, remained beside Max.

"Now *there's* a story!" Max said to the puppy. Max could have wept with joy, but he hid his emotions. "That's a story I was told when I was a wee pup like you."

A few of the dozing dogs had each opened one eye and were watching Max and the runt, clearly curious. Max didn't care who was awake and listening; this one tiny puppy was all the audience he needed.

*"A long, long time ago, your ancestor Rescipius, known as Respi for short, lived in a big city on the other side of the big mountains."* Max

points to the mountains south of the village. *"The city was near a large body of water, and this place was toasty warm all year round. It was called Rome. Respi grew up in a big marble palace with many columns and arches. Many people lived there. They dressed lightly in fluttering gowns. Their feet wore leather sandals that made squeaking noises as they walked around the palace. The men frequently gathered in the marble halls, or in the tiled bath houses where they soaked in soothing warm water, and did a lot of talking.*

*"Respi's master was called Caesar, and he took Respi with him everywhere. Respi very much enjoyed these travels. With Caesar he went on trips south across the big water to a place even warmer than Rome where there were oddly shaped buildings called pyramids. They traveled north over land with an entire army of men and only a few women. Respi had never seen land like this before. The hills back in Rome were anthills compared to what Respi saw as Caesar's army traveled north. And it was cold! With the cold came strange, white stuff that came down from the heavens. When Respi attempted to catch the fluffy white it disappeared in his mouth. It fell to the ground into thick piles and was so cold it hurt Respi's paws.*

*"No matter where they travelled, Caesar made sure Respi was comfortable. Caesar carried Respi under his flowing dress where Respi felt warm and safe. After many days and weeks of travel Caesar's army came to a land where Respi saw humans that smelled and looked very different from Caesar's people. These humans had a strong, refreshing scent (which Respi did not mind at all), and their hair was blond and their eyes icy cold blue like the stuff that came from the heavens.*

*"Much time passed in this northern country, and there was much fighting. Respi did not quite understand why the blond/blue-eyed hu-*

mans were bad or why his master led his army to so fiercely fight them. Throughout all of this warfare, Respi felt safe and protected.

"But then something happened that changed Respi's life. His master, Caesar, when he was not fighting the blondes, began to spend more and more time with one of the blondes. A young girl. Caesar was so in love with the girl he totally ignored and forgot Respi. Respi did not understand why he was ignored and forgotten. Had he been bad, misbehaved in some way?

" If Caesar had ignored and forgotten Respi back in their homeland, in Rome, Respi would have been able to find solace and companionship within his own clan. But here in the town of Rottweil, Respi had never seen one of his own clan. There were other animals of his kind, but their looks and habits were distasteful to Respi, and he never went close enough to realize that their scent was not any different than the dogs of his clan at home. Some of these animals looked vicious, almost like what was called lupus and roamed the forests around Rome. Others looked outright ridiculous: Mother Nature seemed to have forgotten to use the measuring stick when she designed these creatures, as their bodies were longer than their legs. Yet another kind of local mongrel, which Respi only saw once when he was high up in the snowy mountains, looked like a burly, shaggy, stunted cow. Respi wanted nothing to do with these animals and preferred to be lonely rather than associate with such misfits. So during these endlessly long and lonely days, to stop his feelings of disgust and disenchantment, Respi resorted to, what else? — naps.

"One day Respi was awakened from his nap by loud bustling noises. He woke and realized the soldiers were rushing around preparing to abandon the camp. Respi's heart began beating faster as he thought about leaving this strange place at last. Surely better days were ahead for *him. He stood and trotted about camp and realized to his horror that no efforts were being made to pack up his belongings. Respi's food bowl, collar, leash, and bones were left untouched.*

*"Respi's master, Caesar, finally came and took him aside. Caesar looked Respi in the eyes and explained that he was placing a great responsibility into Respi's great paws: Caesar said Respi was the only one in whose care Erda, his blond girl, would be safe.*

*"Respi watched his master depart the North Country with his army. Respi was more proud than sad to be left behind because he had a great responsibility: to protect Erda. Soon after Caesar's departure, a child was born to Erda, a boy. Respi never left Erda or the boy's side, and he was busy and happy again.*

*"Several years passed. The year was what the humans called 44 BC. This did not mean very much to Respi: months he could understand, but not years. The month was March. Life was uneventful. The boy was growing, Erda was happy, and loyal Respi kept his promise to watch out for his master, Caesar's, blond family. Toward mid-month, however, a feeling came upon Respi which he could not explain. He became restless and could not concentrate on his duties. Respi pointed his nose in all directions until he picked up a scent from the south which, although familiar, he could not quite identify. It was an ominous, unsettling scent, and it stirred in Respi a primal urge to leave the house, the garden, the town, and to head south towards Rome.*

*"Respi had never before encountered a dilemma: he felt he should go to his master, but he had been told to stay here with his master's family. For the first time since Caesar had departed, Respi missed him.*

*"Respi missed Caesar because he was his master and because Caesar was also a master in resolving complicated dilemmas.*

"Respi wanted to go south, but he reminded himself that he was doing what his master asked; he was doing a good job, and everybody in Caesar's family was happy. Everyone except Respi.

"It was time for the family to welcome in the New Year. Respi was in no mood to join the celebration. It was a small celebration because only Respi's intimate family celebrated on this date, not the whole town. Respi could never understand why their New Year began in a different month from the rest of the village of Rottweil. Respi, after managing to suppress his primal desire to leave and travel south, escaped the confusing world of humans in a long, deep sleep.

"About one moon had passed. Respi made his rounds through his territory and then stretched out in the stable. Thoughts rambled through his head. He hoped that the year ahead would be a good one for all of his family and that the feeling of doom would soon be lifted from him. He hoped that his master would return to Rottweil and meet his son whom Respi guarded and watched over.

"Respi's thoughts were interrupted by the sounds of hooves. He went out of the stable and saw a soldier, a Roman. Respi wagged his tail in recognition. Could it be that his wishes were coming true so soon in the New Year? The Roman soldier dismounted. The soldier was carrying a puppy just as Caesar had carried Respi when he was a puppy. The young bitch looked very much like the image Respi saw of himself reflected back in the lake.

"The young puppy jumped out from under the soldier's cloak and gracefully landed on the ground by the horse. The soldier left her there and went quickly into the house and closed the door. The soldier was in such a hurry he did not even notice that he had shut the door on the young bitch's face. Respi waited outside with the puppy. A few minutes passed and when the door was finally reopened, Erda emerged from the house holding her young son and crying.

"The message spread fast throughout the household: far to the south in Rome, Respi's master, Caesar, had been stabbed to death on the Ides of March.

"Respi was overwhelmed with remorse and regret. If he had only followed his instincts! Respi was sure if he had been with his master he could have prevented this tragedy.

"Respi was inconsolable. The bitch, called Renata, Rena for short, tried her best to pull Respi out of his sad and sorry state. It was only when Rena told Respi that she soon had to return to Rome with the soldier that Respi snapped out of his mourning for Caesar. He had grown accustomed to Rena's company. He had to find a way to keep her in Rottweil.

"Rena, like Respi, liked Rome far better than the country of the blue-eyed blondes. But she had come to like Respi, too. And as the soldier was not really Rena's master — she told Respi, she never really had a master — Rena happily agreed to hide in the barn until the soldier was gone, just in case he intended to act like her master and take her back to Rome with him.

"The soldier departed the village without Rena, and Rena became Respi's bride. They were a good match. And Rena was very happy. Respi was glad that Rena had stayed. Even so, Rena, who was very perceptive, soon noticed that Respi kept to himself more and more and did not sleep well, both signs of great concern for any dog.

"Rena pondered Respi's mood. Their life was very good — they were already blessed with their third litter — so Rena decided that Respi's sadness must have to do with his master's sudden and violent demise.

*"Another year passed, and Respi remained despondent. Rena was a young bitch, but she nevertheless was streetwise. The following year on the Ides of March, Rena gathered all their children, some of which had found homes with other families in the town, and prepared a celebration in memory of Respi's beloved master. Rena told the clan, now known as the Rottweiler clan, that this year's will be the last memorial for Caesar. Every year hereafter, she explained, there will be a celebration but it will be called R-Day. All of the village dogs will be invited to join in festivities, and all will be merry.*

*"Upon hearing Rena's pronouncement of a new tradition, Respi's cloud of sadness lifted. From that day on, Respi spent most of his time planning and preparing for the next celebration, and Rena took over the daily chores. Respi and Rena lived to be very old dogs, and, surrounded by their family in Rottweil, they remained happy until the end of their long lives."*

Max finished the story he had waited years to tell and looked about the village square. To Max's amazement, none of the dogs had fallen asleep. All of the dogs were alert and listening to his every word.

"So R-Day is the Ides of March to humans?" asked the puppy still seated beside Max.

Max looked down at the little pup. "Yes."

"But why is it called R-Day among the dogs?"

"My grandfather told me that Rena chose that name to honor the town of Rottweil. Other storytellers say Rena called it thus to honor Respi. Long ago, the females of the pack claimed the holiday was named for Rena, because without Rena's wisdom and initiative, there would be no celebration for dogs."

"Whom do you think it was named for?" the puppy asked.

All of the dogs in the square waited for their old leader's response. Finally Max answered:

"I believe it is *Our* Day, a day to celebrate all dogs, and our loyalty, dedication and unconditional love to our masters."

# APRIL
## Eternity

I AM SURE MOST READERS have, like me, pondered what eternity is. I decided to ask my friends and colleagues for their thoughts about eternity. I also consulted the writings of great thinkers. But it was in the eyes of my dog that I found a satisfying answer.

*Northern New Mexico*

Have you ever asked yourself what eternity means? And if so, do you find it daunting, puzzling, enthralling? Perhaps you could not care less?

It was early spring, and my master was rattling off questions (see September story for more examples of this human behavior) and talking to me about something I know very little about: eternity. I knew that it was very important to her, these questions about eternity, because she decided to ask her friends and acquaintances from all walks of life, from all around the world, what they thought about eternity. It seemed that eternity was the only topic my master and her friends could talk about.

I listened to them day and night, in the kitchen, on the porch, over the phone, talking about what eternity might be. I did not understand what all the excitement was about, nor did I particularly care. For a dog, eternity is a fairly simple concept best explained by examples: waiting for supper, waiting for master to wake up or come home; this is eternity. However, among humans the question as to what is eternity provokes an astounding array and diversity of answers.

"It is timelessness and/or everlastingness," said one of my master's erudite friends. Erudite means scholarly and learned, at least among humans. For dogs, an erudite master means the house is filled to capacity and beyond with books, and the master (like mine) spends many *many* hours sitting in a chair reading a book or paper and scribbling in a notebook. This is accompanied by her staring into space and pondering things unseen by a dog. All of this studious activity is followed by the master's questions and by what often seems like aimless and endless conversation with her dog and herself.

"Nothingness," said another of my master's friends, "eternity means nothingness." Nothing, to my way of thinking, which is a dog's way of thinking, can be understood best by images: a bowl without food, a sky without clouds, a bucket with no water. These are examples of nothing. No thing in the bowl or the bucket. No thing in the sky. Empty. Nothingness is some thing with the characteristics of no thing.

"I am puzzled and amazed by eternity but don't know what it is," said an honest friend. My master nodded thoughtfully to this friend's response, but I do not believe it satisfied my master's quest for an answer. They were having tea in the living room, and the friend didn't stay long. After the friend left, my master put away the tea cups, pulled out a wine glass and a bottle of a good French red, and returned to her ruminating and mumbling with me, her most loyal friend, at her side.

"I would have to bring God into this conversation," said a non-committal friend, "and I don't want to."

I'm pretty sure my master would have liked her non-committal friend to bring God into the conversation, but my master didn't press for it. My master is a gentle person. She only becomes agitated when the questions she's pondering are not gentle.

"Eternity is an Irish rock group," said a girlfriend that came to the house and walked around with plugs in her ears. My master is not given to rolling her eyes, but I'm pretty certain I saw her brown eyes roll about their sockets. However, my master did not let her girlfriend see her momentary lapse in decorum. Like me, my master is very polite.

A friend who loves to sing while she works in the garden said, or rather sang, "Eternity is forever-morica." My master laughed but did not sing along.

Later that day, my master's cultured but aloof dance teacher sent an email: "E - 6h." My master contemplated this cryptic message for a few minutes and then called her dance teacher who lives on the other side of the world.

"Are you saying that eternity is six hours en pointe?" I could not hear the dance teacher's response. After a long pause, my master said into the telephone, "Yes, six hours in a dentist's chair would qualify for eternity in any language!"

My master hung up the phone, looked at me, and sighed.

"Plato said, 'Time is the moving image of eternity.'" My master was sitting at her desk when she turned to me and quoted this guy Plato. I have never before heard my master mention the name Plato, so he cannot be a close friend. Good thing, because if this person were to come over and have tea with my master, I'm pretty sure his opinions and statements — although lovely to the ear — would be the cause of even more restless ruminating and late-night mumbling by my master.

My master's mother came over and sat in the kitchen talking with my master. She held me on her lap and petted my head and told my master: "I wanted to name you Eternity because you were so long overdue and just did not seem to want to come into this world."

My master smiled. I wonder: had my master been named Eternity, would she have a better understanding of eternity? Probably not; humans have difficulties understanding themselves.

The search for an answer continued. "Eternity is a consolation for our short time on this earth," an always optimistic friend said. We were out walking, and my master asked her friend something about the hereafter, and soon they were discussing an entirely different topic with a whole different set of questions. At least this conversation distracted my master from her eternity (eternal) quest for a few hours.

"Don't kill the short time you have on this earth," a pessimistic, dour friend told my master. "This could possibly hurt or alter eternity." I hoped my master would ask how one could possibly kill something you cannot see, smell, touch, hear, or find? But the pessimistic friend left my master's house almost as quickly as her honest friend had a few days before.

At a dinner party, a friend dressed in flowing robes sat beside my master. During the first course (humans are often served more than one bowl of food per meal) he said, "I thought to serve eternity tonight." My master stopped eating and stared into space. I settled down onto my rug and prepared for a good sleep. I knew this would be a long dinner party now that someone had brought up eternity.

Another friend at the dinner table said, "If you love for only a hundredth of a second, you have stolen from eternity." My master called the friend a romantic. The friend said she was still waiting for 'it' to happen. I tried to fall asleep at my master's feet, but I could not; what was 'it' and how could the best thing in the world — love — steal from something no human yet understands?

"Eternity is something we are in it at the moment," the assistant at the vet's office told my master. "But you don't know what it is." Now really, I was very fond and appreciative of the people at the vet's office, but I thought the assistant had stepped well beyond his professional arena when he suggested my master 'did not know what it is.' He had obviously not given eternity the time and thought that my master had. And if it is something we are in at this moment, then why wouldn't we know what it is?!

The vet assistant's lofty but ultimately empty declaration was to be the first of many. I learned that many humans speak with great authority and confidence about things they have never thought about.

"Don't look at your watch for eternity." This was spoken by one of my master's glib colleagues, a man who wore fitted suits and silk scarves, and who brought me chocolates that I was never allowed to eat. My master liked this comment, but she still did not let me have any of the chocolates.

"What a waste of time to think about eternity." This statement, given by a neighbor who rebuilds automobiles and does not like dogs, ended his relationship with my master. I do not believe, however, that he knows their relationship has ended. Although he is a very good mechanic, my master says he is eternally dim-witted.

I could go on and on. I said before that I was amazed at the variety and diversity of answers gathered in my master's quest for an understanding of eternity. Her search took her deeply into the quagmire, what we dogs would call a bog. Imagine stepping into quicksand and then trying to get out. This is where my master's quest led her. The more she struggled for an answer, the deeper she sunk into her quandary.

I do not like to see my master suffer. What she needed is a down-to-earth answer that only a dog can provide. I waited and waited for my master to ask ME for the answer to her question. Finally, one bright morning in early spring before she had her coffee or read the newspaper, my master looked down at me and asked: "How long is eternity?"

I sat up and wagged and wagged my tail. I had waited so long for this moment.

"Simple," I answered. "It is twice as long as half of eternity."

My master laughed, picked me up, and said, "April Fool!"

# MAY
# The Golden Dog of the Madres

IN 2003, THE COMPLETE human genome data were released to the world. As life starts as a single cell, each carrying identical DNA, the obvious next question was how these cells do differentiate into brain cells, muscle cells, liver cells, etc. What are the factors that control the expression of the genes without changing the gene? After the announcement in 2003, a race began in the scientific community to develop a library of the epigenome, i.e., all the factors that control the expression of the genes without changing the genes, i.e., the sequence of the DNA. Another, even more enticing question remained unresolved: can qualities acquired by behavior be transmitted to the next generation? In this story it is a dog that provides decisive proof that transgenerational epigenetic inheritance (non-genetic transmission to the future offspring) indeed takes place.

*Buenos Aires, Argentina*

Analucia was the offspring of a morganatic union between a mongrel father and an aristocratic mother; a misalliance it was, in a world where such socializing between the classes was frowned upon. From the very moment Analucia was born, her life was different from those of her litter mates. Analucia was the only puppy in the litter that resembled the mongrel father. So while her brothers and sisters remained where they were born in a beautiful residence in Recoleta, Analucia, the only mongrel puppy, was removed from her mother, taken to the nearby park, and left to die.

It was August, winter in Buenos Aires, and Analucia was very hungry and very cold. She fell asleep thinking that this would be a sleep that would last forever, and was soon dreaming about a big white bird carrying her cold little body toward the warm sun. But when Analucia opened her eyes, she found herself held by two scarred, rough, but oh so warm hands. She would not remember much more about that first day with her family — only that she was very hungry and very cold and that the family rescued her from certain death.

Analucia was carried to a narrow back-street, and to a small, dark tent-like home where there was warm milk, small children holding her, and music in the distance. Analucia was taken in and adopted by a poor, but happy family in San Telmo, a barrio of Buenos Aires. Here she lived a carefree life. The scraps of food that the family saved for her were delicious and plenty enough for Analucia to gain weight. She became a statuesque, strong, and pretty mongrel dog. The parents were gone during the day, working and making a living. Analucia accompanied the children to the park and to school or just watched them play in the street near their tiny home. Not having experienced luxury, Analucia believed she was living in a fine castle with the king and queen and their young princess and two princes.

Life was good for Analucia and her family — at least until that horrible day in 1979. The father had left for work, and the mother was home doing chores and cleaning the house. There was a knock on the door, and two tall, slender men in uniform came into the house. The soldiers talked with the mother. Analucia listened; it seemed friendly enough at first. Suddenly it was not friendly; the mother began to shriek and the men's faces turned fierce. The mother screamed and struggled to gather and hold her children, but the soldiers were too strong for her; they pulled away two of the three children and ran out the door.

Analucia ran after them barking and snapping at their ankles. She bit into the leg of one of the soldiers, but he kicked Analucia and she flew like a wingless bird through the air and landed hard on the concrete. Analucia struggled to get up and continue her pursuit, but she could not stand on one of her hind legs. She buckled and cried out as pain ran up through her leg. Analucia was tough — she had experienced mental pain — but she had never known pain like this. Analucia could not run; she could barely stand. She lay on the ground helplessly watching as the mother, screaming hysterically, ran after the soldiers who had taken her two children. The men pushed the children into a military car and disappeared.

Analucia watched as the mother ran after the car, waving her arms, screaming out in the street, all to no avail. After a long while the mother returned to the house. Analucia crawled home and lay down near the mother who sat in her rocking chair. She rocked for hours, staring at nothing. At dusk the father came home. When he saw his wife, he knew what had happened. He had heard from his neighbors and friends similar stories, but he was shocked that this could happen to his family. They were good citizens, were honest, hard-working people. They never harmed anyone or anything.

From this time on, life was different. No more laughter in the house, only sad faces. The little boy who was left behind no longer played out of doors in the park. Analucia felt guilty. Maybe it had all been her fault? Why couldn't she stop the soldiers from taking the two children? They had guns. They were strong.

Analucia missed the children; she missed their scent, their caresses, cuddling and sleeping with them. Analucia's only light, her one consolation, was that the bereaved mother left all of the children's clothes strewn around the little house exactly as they had left them. She did not wash the missing children's clothing. The mother wanted the house to remain as it was when they were a happy family.

Analucia, like the mother, liked to be surrounded by the children's things. Analucia sat close to their toys, and she particularly liked to lie down on their clothes. The scent of the kidnapped children remained strong in Analucia. She would never, ever forget them and how they smelled. And the master never took away the sweet smelling clothing of the lost children.

Years passed. Analucia was getting up in age. The family's only son had grown into a young man. He didn't play with Analucia anymore. One day Analucia decided to visit the park where the children used to play when there were three of them in the family. Analucia was hoping to pick up the scent of the kidnapped children, a scent she never forgot even though only a few tattered pieces of the children's clothing remained in her bed.

Analucia was a good tracker (a skill inherited from her father the mongrel), but she could not pick up a scent of the children. After sitting in the park for an hour, Analucia turned and limped for home. She was thinking of nothing in particular when a handsome dog emerged in the corner of her eye. He approached Analucia. She was in heat and so did not mind this male approaching her. Analucia's sad mood lifted. He was a beautiful dog. Analucia knew he could help her produce beautiful puppies. Analucia and the male dog became lovers, at least for a short time. Analucia had never experienced this kind of love.

Analucia arrived back at the home of her family feeling both guilty and happy. The next day she returned to the park again with great expectations, but the handsome dog was not there. Actually, she realized those feelings she had for him had begun to wane. As Analucia wandered toward her home, she wondered how people can be lovers for months, even years.

Soon Analucia had no desire to go out and see the male dog again. She only wanted to stay home, eating, sleeping. Walking became more difficult and tiresome, and, even though Analucia did not eat more than before, she gained weight and became very round. She felt movement in her tummy, kicking, and turning. Analucia felt happy. She did not even protest when her master removed the remnants of the lost children's clothing and replaced them with clean rags.

One bright morning Analucia brought three creatures into the world. Two girls and one boy. Alas, the girls did not move and no amount of Analucia's licking could put breaths into their small, wet bodies. But the boy was strong and wiggled immediately and searched for Analucia's milk. He was welcomed by the whole family, and he brought new life into the house.

The family named Analucia's puppy Lito, short for Rafaelito. Analucia nursed him with great affection, and he grew into a handsome dog that was taken everywhere, just like Analucia when she was young. Lito grew into a strong dog. But as he became stronger,

Analucia became weaker. Her aging slowed her down, and soon she spent most of her time sleeping in the bed that she shared with Lito.

Lito particularly like to accompany the mother of the family to the city every week. She gathered with other women at the Plaza de Mayo. All of the women wore a white scarf on their heads, and lined up and walked around some monument carrying a banner. For the first few months at the plaza Lito was hidden under the mother's sweater so that he would not get trampled or lost.

Analucia passed away in the middle of the night. Lito said his goodbyes to his mother and then her body was taken away. Life went on in the family. Lito was now a large, handsome dog, and he walked proudly ahead of the Madres of the Plaza de Mayo, as they were called. Lito did not quite understand the purpose of these gatherings on the plaza, but the women, all mothers, seemed to share a common sadness. They wanted to remind the people of Buenos Aires of an event that had happened years ago. An event that happened when Lito's mother, Analucia, was a young dog.

One day on the plaza a familiar scent caught Lito's attention. Lito, who now always walked out ahead of the Madres, strayed from the line of women and followed the scent over to a group of people standing on the side of the plaza. The scent grew in intensity. Lito followed it to a young man. The Madres were watching Lito, and, when he stood in front of the young man, they lost their slow, rhythmical gait and stopped. Lito had never left the line, never done anything like this.

Lito's master left the women and followed Lito. She began to run until she caught up with him, breathless and upset. She stood beside Lito in front of the young man and looked up at his face. She studied it very carefully. A feeling came over Lito's master, a feeling buried deep down in her heart for many years. She said, "He looks just like my husband did when he was young."

Lito jumped up and licked the young man. Lito felt he had known this young man all his life. The mother, too, felt something very magical happening inside her. She knew this young man. He knew, too.

Slowly, Lito's master found her voice. Words were spoken. Who are you? Why are you here? How old are you? Where did you grow up? The young man said that he and his sister, who was not with him that day at the plaza, grew up in a military family. They knew they had been adopted. They did not know where or how. And now, because they intended to start families of their own, the siblings had tried to find their biological mother. But thus far, their efforts had been to no avail.

It is the year 2010, and much time has passed since the horrible day when the master's children were taken. Much has happened outside the small world Lito lives in. Even so, this moment on the plaza is a turning point in the history of people and dogs.

This singular, seemingly insignificant moment between a dog and a young man, and the story of one of the anonymous Madres in the Plaza de Mayo, was picked up by a reporter and published in the city's largest newspaper. And faster than Lito could comprehend the life around his family changed. DNA analysis was done that proved that the young man had indeed found his biological mother. And the scientists became interested in Lito. How was this dog able to identify the son of his master? The dog was not alive when his master's son was taken from the family home. And the kidnapped son had no recollection of his mother.

Finally, a plausible explanation came from a renowned scientist, Dr. Evita Appleton, who lived in a country far away on another continent. Dr. Appleton flew to Buenos Aires to meet Lito. Dr. Appleton explained that, although the clothes were taken before Lito was born, the scent of the lost children had affected the development of Lito's brain. Because Lito's mother, Analucia, for years would not allow anyone in the family to remove the clothing of the kidnapped children, Lito was exposed to the scent as an embryo. The scent of those children had been passed from Analucia to her puppy, Lito, in the womb. Even before Dr. Appleton had studied Lito and his family, she had given it a name, "transgenerational epigenetic inheritance."

Unbeknown to Lito, before she left Argentina, Dr. Appleton requested that when Lito was ready to begin his journey into dog heaven, she be given his brain to study. Lito probably would have been proud that his brain was so important to science. But for now, Lito remains ignorant of his future importance.

Sometimes it is better not to know everything. As an old proverb says: "Talk is silver; silence is golden."

Whether in this life or in the hereafter, at the Plaza de Mayo, Lito will be remembered as the golden dog.

# JUNE
## Old Pekka and the Dreadful Bird

I ATTENDED A CONFERENCE in Finland in June, a time of year when it is never completely dark in that part of the world. While I had no problems sleeping because I could close the curtains and darken my hotel room, the birds outside my window could not. Unable to sleep, they chirped all night. It started out as a happy chirp, but their songs quickly turned into what sounded like screeching. I thought at the time how the birds in Scandinavian countries must become extremely neurotic during this time of endless day, endless light.

*Rauma, Finland*

Old Pekka is too tired to hold up his head. He must drag his old, bony body home from his daily visit to the coast. In his master's native language, Finnish, Pekka's name means rock. Today Pekka wonders if perhaps he ought to act like a rock and settle down in one place? Even though it is difficult for Pekka to walk so far, every morning he still goes across the fields to the sea with the hope that he will find his master coming in from a night of fishing.

Of course, his master did not come in at dawn when all the other fishermen brought in their catches. Pekka's master hasn't come in with the other fishermen in years. But Pekka's memories are deep and the remembrance of the good old days when he went out on the boat before sunrise with his master, and the hope that his master will come back one day and ask him to come along again, gives Pekka the energy to make the journey to the coast every morning.

It occurs to Pekka that if his master were to come back, it might be too late for Pekka. Pekka is no longer the strong, muscular dog that went out on the boat. His gouty body would have to be lifted in and out of master's boat, and his balance would be terrible if the waves were high. Would his company alone be sufficient to please his master?

Pekka walks slowly away from the sea and back to the modest house where his master's children live. They treat him well. They feed Pekka good food and have built a nice house for him under the big linden tree in the corner of the garden. Pekka's life is comfortable, but solitary. He misses being needed. He misses being loved.

Although it is light all day and all night, Pekka still keeps the same hours for his waking and sleeping. Pekka loves this time of the year. No matter how old he is, or how tired, the long days in June always manage to raise his spirits. After returning from his customary walk to the coast, Pekka crawls into his house, settles down onto his comfortable bed, and sighs deeply. His whole body is ready for a long nap. But just as the wonderful feeling of sleep begins to seep into his bones and muscles, Pekka hears a voice. An irritating, squeaky voice that comes from the top of the linden tree near Pekka's house. The little voice repeats over and over the same words: "Dreadful, dreadful, how dreadful!"

Pekka reluctantly opens his eyes and lifts his heavy head. Who would disturb Pekka during one of the few pleasures left in old Pekka's life, his sleep? Pekka was looking forward to sinking into his favorite dream, a dream in which he runs like a Greyhound — those dogs with legs like horses and bodies long and lean, made for endless chasing — toward something. Pekka does not exactly know what he is running toward in this dream — just that it is something wonderful, and that he is very fast and never tires. Pekka always wakes refreshed and energized after this running dream.

So it is with great reluctance that Pekka shakes off the good feeling of a nap coming on, opens his eyes and looks around to search for the origin of the squeaky voice. He goes to the door of his house and looks up and spots a small bird fidgeting up and down on a narrow branch close to the crown of the tree. The bird continues to mumble the same words over and over in a garbled voice: "Dreadful, dreadful, how dreadful."

Pekka stands under the tree and says up to the bird: "Get a hold of yourself and go to sleep. Or find yourself another tree. You are disturbing my nap."

The bird stops his monotonous chanting and peers down at Pekka standing in the doorway of the dog house.

"Easy for you; you are a dog," the bird says. "You can sleep any place, any time, day or night. But it has not been night for days. I need the darkness to close my eyes. I cannot go on much longer."

The bird wobbles on the branch and flaps its wings for balance. Pekka can see that the bird is desperate.

"I will die unless darkness comes over the sky soon," the bird continues.

Pekka looks up at the bird and says, "What is your name, bird?"

"My name is Sinichka," the bird replies.

"You are not from here?" Pekka asks.

"No, I am from Belarus, where the sun sets, even in summer. Oh why did I come here to live?! Dreadful, dreadful, how dreadful!"

Pekka thinks about this for a moment. "Why don't you fly back to your home in Belarus, Sinichka?"

"Because it is dreadful there, dreadful!" Sinichka shakes her feathers and lifts her exhausted wings. "I cannot go back. It is not a good place to live. I am no fool!"

"Just close your eyes," Pekka suggested. "With your eyes closed, it will be dark. This is what I do to sleep."

"What a dreadful simpleton! Don't you know that this method works for dogs but not for birds?" Sinichka became so agitated she nearly fell from the branch. "Dreadful, dreadful, how dreadful!"

Pekka felt sorry for the dreadful Sinichka who could not sleep. Pekka sat down in the door of his house and thought about the word 'simpleton.' Pekka thinks a simpleton is someone who can simply solve any problem. If Pekka is a simpleton, then he ought to be able to solve this bird's problem. Pekka saw his chance to do a good deed, to be useful — something he has not been in a long time. Maybe he could help the dreadful bird go to sleep, and then he could go to sleep, too. And Pekka would feel good about himself.

Pekka thought and thought until he remembered a wonderful afternoon nap long ago. It was the time he followed his master into a cave one hot Scandinavian summer day. The sun was relentless, and master was hot and thirsty. Inside, the cave was cool, dark, and moist. Master told Pekka to lie down and go to sleep. Master settled down against the cave wall and fell asleep, too. Pekka lay down beside his master, and they slept a long time in the cool cave above the sea. It was heavenly.

Pekka would describe the wonderful feeling of that nap, and Sinichka the bird from Belarus would fall asleep.

"What I remember best is the darkness," Pekka began his story. "It was dark, dark, a dark cave near the sea…"

As Pekka remembered that wonderful summer afternoon, his words became very soft. Soon he was asleep.

"Dreadful, dreadful," Sinichka squeaked from the tree. "How dreadful, this simpleton!"

Pekka, startled by the bird's racket, woke up and continued the story. "Now, where were we? Oh yes, in the dark cave."

"Stop!" Sinichka called out. "I cannot fall asleep thinking of a cold, wet cave where ugly creatures are hanging from the ceiling, dreadful things which are a disgrace to everyone in the flying winged world!"

Pekka apologized to the bird. He was beginning to understand how simple problem-solving was not so easy. After standing and shaking his old body, Pekka sat down again, rested and ready to give this challenging but worthy endeavor another try.

Pekka began a second story:

"There was a white bird with golden wings. The wings were very special because they never tired. The bird's leader, Fredson, soon noticed that this particular member of his flock was unique. Fredson was a good leader and he understood how the white bird's special wings could potentially benefit the whole flock. Fredson had come from a different land. He had heard about a faraway planet seen only at night. This planet was called La Luna in some countries, moon in others. Fredson was told that La Luna was filled with gold. He had also heard, and it made good sense to him, that the guard of the gold, called the Man in the Moon by some, was only watching when there was a full moon. Fredson decided to send the white bird with the golden wings to the moon to steal the gold. He planned to have the white bird fly when the moon was at its smallest.

"Fredson explained the task to the white bird with the golden wings. When the moon was furthest from full, the white bird began its flight to the moon. He flew and flew. It was very far, very far, very far, but the white bird never ever became tired, tired, tired…"

Pekka fell sound asleep. After a short restful nap, Pekka woke up.

"Where were we? Oh, yes, the bird with the golden wings."

"Dreadful, dreadful, how dreadful!" Sinichka was more exasperated than before Pekka fell asleep. "How can I sleep listening to such dreadful nonsense? How can La Luna have a guard called the Man in the Moon? How can the moon increase one day, decrease another, be there one day, gone another?! What nonsense! I will never sleep! It is hopeless. I should not listen to you, simpleton! Stop! Stop!"

Pekka lay down in his doorway and placed his heavy head on his old paws. He was very discouraged. If only the dreadful little bird had shown a little more patience, he would have fallen asleep for sure. If Pekka had been able to finish the story, he could have told the bird about how the white bird with the golden wings flew to the other side of the moon where it was dark as night all the time. A place where a bird could sleep as long as she wanted.

Sinichka marched up and down her branch chanting her dreadful words. Pekka, feeling like a failure, went back into his house. He had never felt so dejected and old. Pekka moaned and sighed, groaned and grunted. Pekka could not sleep. He tossed and turned on his blankets, sighed and moaned, and turned again. It was a dreadful sound — Pekka unable to sleep in his dog house.

Sinichka could hear the sounds of Pekka's sleepless agitation. Pekka never had trouble sleeping. The bird felt sorry and guilty for being so rough and rude, as if her problems could be blamed on the old dog.

"I have to console this nice, gentle creature," Sinichka thought. Instead of chanting her dreadful words, the bird called down to Pekka: "Hey, dog, I am sorry."

No answer. Sinichka flew off her branch down to the entrance of the dog house. The dog did not move but sulked with his old bony back turned toward the entrance.

"I want to talk with you," the bird said kindly. "Turn around."

No answer. Sinichka needed to do something very big. She hopped in through the door and over the dog to the far corner of the dog house. Once Sinichka's eyes became accustomed to the darkness, she moved closer to Pekka. To Sinichka's surprise a tear rolled down Pekka's cheek.

"What have I done?" the bird thought. "I am a thankless, dreadful creature."

Sinichka looked about Pekka's house. There was nothing dreadful in the dog's house! The bird had not felt so secure, so warm, and so *sleepy* since she left her parents' nest a long time ago.

"What is your name, dog?" Sinichka asked.

"Pekka."

"Pekka, you have a wonderful home. May I share it with you?"

Pekka moved his old body and made room for the bird. And Sinichka the bird from Belarus snuggled up to the shaggy, warm old Pekka and fell fast asleep. She even began to snore — just a soft bird snore that was like music to Pekka's ears. Pekka felt the good feeling of a nap moving in, the dream of endless running coming toward him. But before he fell asleep, Pekka felt another tear leave his old eye and run down his nose. This was a tear of happiness. Not even in dreams had old Pekka felt so needed, loved, and happy.

# JULY
## The Dogs Who Lived Between
## a Rock and a Hard Place

As FAR BACK AS I CAN REMEMBER, I have loved music, particularly operas. At the age of eleven, I locked myself into my room to listen to Wagner operas sent from Bayreuth. The static of my small transistor radio was a minor nuisance compared to the pleasure the music gave me.

Anyone who has seen or heard the "Ring of the Nibelungs" knows about the absurd behavior of the operas' gods, heroes and mythical figures. It occurred to me that my dog who endures these operas with me knows nothing about revenge, vengeance, and reckoning — a common theme throughout the Ring. Wagner is known to have been devoted to his pets: Russ, his Newfoundland, is buried next to the composer and was supposedly the only critic Wagner valued; and Peps, a stray the composer picked up in Riga, is said to have helped Wagner compose "Tannhäuser."

Wagner's stories have plenty of revenge, but I do not believe Wagner ever incorporated dogs into any of his operas. Therefore, for our dog story about revenge and reckoning we turn to the Greek myth of Skylla.

*The Strait of Messina, Italy*

My master likes to read to me on long summer evenings in July. I listen, but I don't always understand. Often I am bored and take a little nap, even though she continues to read to me. I don't let her know that I am bored, or napping. I sit beside her with my head on her feet or her lap. I guess reading to me, and talking to me about what she's reading, helps my master to sort out things she's thinking about (humans do a lot of thinking) and to ponder complicated ideas and concepts.

When my master is reading or thinking about what she's reading, she asks me questions — a *lot* of questions. She doesn't ask easy questions (she knows how intelligent dogs are). For instance, my master recently asked me about God: What is God, where is God, and what does He look like? She asked me if there is more than one God? Does He (if indeed He is a he) watch out for all of us? For me, for you, for all animals and plants? Is God always good, or can He be evil? Can one choose a God, or are we stuck with the God(s) that are part of the culture into which we are born and live? She even asked me who *created* God.

I look at my master as she asks these questions and pretend that I know at least a few of the answers. My wisdom, be it real or imagined, must somehow be transmitted to her (perhaps through my kind eyes), because after my master has talked with me for a while she usually looks rather pleased. She pets me and thanks me for being such a fine companion. And then she gets up and goes on about her day, goes out in her car to run errands or visit friends. I assume my master has found the answers to at least a few of her questions. Little does she know that after these readings and conversations, I end up hopelessly baffled and bewildered about the scope and complexity of human preoccupation. And left alone in the house, I have nothing to distract me from worrying and ruminating and obsessively chewing over (because I am a dog) the many stories, ideas, and questions my master has shared with me.

For example, I was told disturbing stories about the gods that are found (well, not exactly found; my master says not even a good hound dog could track and find these gods) in Greece, in Rome, in the Nordic world, in Egypt, in India, China, and Japan. I am sure there are countries or continents I have left out. Many of these gods are cruel; they harm other gods, their own wives, their children, and all mortals for all manner of petty and grand crimes: murder, incest, adultery, kidnapping, even cannibalism. We dogs know what is good and bad, what is right and wrong. We also understand forgiveness (how else could we cohabitate with humans for so many, many centuries?). But there are human responses one person to another that we dogs do not understand — for instance, revenge.

This reminds me of the ending to a story my master read to me: "Revenge is like biting a dog because he bit you." She said this is the moral to the story. But because I do not understand revenge, I do not precisely understand the moral. After giving this moral a summer afternoon of thought, I said to myself, 'Guess who is the fool here?' Not the dog. But I digress.

I want to please my master and be a good listener when she reads aloud and talks to me. But if I am a good listener, it may mean I am left to contemplate human dilemmas for which I have no answer or understanding. I have heard my master refer to predicaments such as this as 'being between a rock and a hard place.'

Now I *do* understand that story! I will share this Greek myth, as my master calls it, with my fellow canines because although it is a human story the heroes are dogs.

In Old Greece there was a beautiful maiden named Skylla. She was the daughter of the River Goddess Krataiis. (In Greek mythology strange things happened.) Skylla was loved by Glaukos, the God of the Sea. But, alas, (my master says 'alas' when telling me

Greek myths) another goddess, a witch named Circe, loved Glaukos. Circe wanted Glaukos to love her, not Skylla. But Glaukos scorned Circe, which means he did not return her love. This hurt and humiliated Circe, and, in an angry, jealous rage, she poisoned the sea where Skylla liked to go and bathe. When Skylla waded into the poisoned water of the sea, her slender legs and lovely lower body were hideously transformed into six vile hound-heads and twelve dog legs.

The once beautiful and kind Skylla turned into a fearsome monster. Yelping hideously, she fled (on her twelve dog legs) away from the sea she had once loved. The ugly monster Skylla retreated to a cave on one side of the Strait of Messina between Calabria and Sicily. From this rocky perch, Skylla vented her rage and hate and plotted her revenge.

On the other side of the Strait of Messina was a second monster called Charybdis. Charybdis had a single gaping mouth. When Charybdis took in a deep breath through her horrible mouth, it created mammoth, dangerous whirlpools in the sea.

As goddesses turned sea-monsters, Skylla and Charybdis posed a double danger to sailors and their boats passing through the Strait of Messina. If a sailor went too close to Charybdis, his boat was destroyed and the sailor drowned in Charybdis' mighty whirlpools; if a sailor tried to escape Charybdis' violent whirlpools and steered his boat close to the rocky cliffs where Skylla waited, he was caught in Skylla's revenge-seeking arms and eaten by the dogs that were Skylla's lower body.

"They had to choose between a rock and a hard place," my master said. "You can see how there was no good choice. Either way, the sailors lost."

Odysseus, the Greek king despised by the Romans after he defeated them in the Trojan Wars, although warned by Circe of the wrath of Skylla, lost six of his seamen to the ferocious jaws of Skylla's six dogs. Skylla and her dogs, it seems, were more cunning than the legendary king.

After years of Skylla's rage was vented on sailors passing through the Strait of Messina, one of the six dogs, today remembered as Calliah, lost her appetite and desire to feast on innocent sailors. Nowadays, Calliah is the name given to a homely dog with a beautiful soul. In Old Greece, Calliah was just a name for one of Skylla's six dog heads. Calliah was ugly, but she was smart. And her soul although never seen was beautiful.

In the many dozens of quiet, uneventful days when no sailors or ships strayed close to Skylla's rocks, Calliah thought about how Circe was jealous and Skylla wanted revenge. While dogs know all about jealousy, we do not know anything at all about revenge. Calliah pondered how she had come to be a dog seeking revenge and how confusing it all was, being part of a goddess turned monster, all tangled up in a human body with five other dogs.

And this is when Calliah's beautiful soul, all but lost in the ugly body of Skylla, began to emerge. Calliah's innate canine wisdom came up with a solution that promised to bring peace to all that passed through the Strait of Messina, the place where the sea passed between the rock and the hard place.

Calliah had to re-awaken in her brothers and sisters the characteristics inherent in their canine genes — forgiveness and clemency — and also abolish the foreign characteristic that Skylla had instilled in them — revenge. To do this, Calliah began to tell stories to her canine siblings about dogs all over the world — how they loved their masters who gave them food and shelter. Calliah told stories that explained to her dog family how confusing and misguided humans could be sometimes, causing them to behave badly towards dogs and one another. She also shared stories about the gods and goddesses who could also be especially nasty toward one another as well as toward the human and animal world. All of Calliah's stories helped her brothers and sisters remember that dogs have great hearts and are born to love and serve — not to hate and attack.

As they learned from Calliah's stories about the true nature of canines, the dogs of Skylla agreed amongst themselves that they wanted no part of Skylla's revenge.

From that day on they refused Skylla's order to kill and eat sailors who strayed too close to their side of the Strait. Calliah warned them that their decision could cause Skylla to take revenge on them. But Skylla did not turn her wrath on the dogs. Instead, Skylla, perhaps as weary of her vengeful behavior as the dogs, changed from a mean beast back to the calm and placid girl she used to be. Skylla no longer showed any interest in the sea, and in the ships and the sailors passing through the Strait of Messina. All of Skylla's energy was directed to the care of her dogs. She went out and gathered the proper food for Calliah and her siblings and talked to them while she groomed and caressed them. Life for the dogs, and for Skylla, was peaceful and good.

Calliah would have been perfectly content if their life had continued this way forever. But one afternoon Skylla fell into a very deep sleep. No matter what the dogs did to rouse her — licking her face, nipping her fingers, barking, nudging, tugging — their beloved master Skylla did not wake up. After several days in a deep slumber, Skylla's upper body turned to stone. And when this happened the six dogs were released from her torso and transformed into six beautiful animals.

Today, Skylla still sleeps peacefully on top of the rock protected by her six loyal dogs. Sailors have continued to pass unscathed between the rock and the hard place — the Strait of Messina — for thousands of years. Thanks to the wisdom and good sense of Calliah, the homely dog with the beautiful heart, sailors may travel safely as long as they stay on the calm and placid side of the sea that belongs to Skylla and her beloved dogs.

# AUGUST
## Drums for My Oba

A TRIP TO THE YORUBALAND, a cultural region in southwest Nigeria, opened my eyes to a completely new and unfamiliar civilization. I was particularly moved by the music and dancing. Accompanied by a native companion and interpreter, I visited all strata of Yoruba society and was introduced to everyone from beggars to obas (kings). My experiences in Yorubaland were transforming.

*Oshogbo, Nigeria*

MY NAME IS ASHAKE

AJA ASHAKE

THE OBA'S DOG

THE ONE WHO SHIELDS HIM FROM HARM

THE ONE WHO COVERS THE FLOOR WITH ODODO FLOWERS

THE OBA'S DOG

I live in the Oba's palace in Oshogbo. My name, Ashake, means *one who is selected to be spoiled with good things*. I was selected because I have a spot on my face that is the mirror image of the Oba's aristocratic tribal mark. I am beautiful, as beautiful as the most beautiful gazelle.

I was born into the Yoruba tribe, a tribe that honors animals as equals. Paradoxically, the Yoruba believe that we dogs were created to serve. And so we do. I am the Oba's, the King's companion. I am privileged. So are my two friends, the parrot named Aduke, whose name means *people will fight over the privilege to spoil her;* and the vulture Akanni, whose name means *first male child.* You may have noticed that my people, the Yoruba, are not very imaginative. My name and all of my friends' names begin with the letter A. The parrot Aduke, the vulture Akanni, and I, Ashake, the trio of the palace, are treated with great respect. We share not only the pleasures and joys with the Oba but also the pain and misery that he, even though a King, or *because* he is a King, experiences occasionally. We protect him, entertain him, and make him happy.

Our lives in the palace were serene and tranquil for what I believe was many years. I know it was many years because the Oba's wives gave him many children. I watched the Oba's children develop from beautiful babies who crawled all over me, squeezed me, and used me in their attempts to stand up and walk, into proper boys and girls who showed me the deference I deserve as the Oba's aja. I had a soft bed, was served delicious food, and was shown much affection by the Oba and his family.

I never left the Oba's palace except for the big Oshogbo Festival in August. I looked forward to this event all year. It was a break from the isolation we all lived within at the palace. As the Oba's carriage made its way to the festival over bumpy roads, I saw a very different life than what I saw and experienced in the palace. The roads were lined with houses that looked like they could collapse into the earth at any time. And what bothered me most — and please remember I am a dog — was the repulsive stench that rose from the immense piles of trash strewn everywhere on the roads and alongside the houses.

I learned from my Oba to ignore these unpleasant sights and smells. I instead focused upon the lovely trees and flowers, the colorful robes, and the hustle and bustle of what seemed to be happy, healthy people. Although there was a bountiful cornucopia of delicious food and vibrant fabric at the August festival, what I looked forward to most each year was the continuous sound of the drums. Once a year at the palace, the most renowned drummer, an octogenarian from Erin, a little town outside of Oshogbo, came and played for the King on his birthday. But the rest of the year, the palace was rather quiet.

I must be a reincarnation of the dog of the Yoruba deity of music because my love of music, particularly drumming, is exceptional. I am drawn to the sounds of the *ashiko, djembe, dundun,* and *bata.* I know and love them all. The drums stir something deep and primal in me that I cannot explain. I even feel the Talking Drums produce my name, Ah-sh-a-ke. I wish I could dance, but it is not proper for the dog of the Oba to dance. So, I dance with my eyes closed. *Oma bi bu, oma bi bu, oma bi bu oba,* over and over.

One year the Oba of another province visited our palace. When this visiting Oba saw me, he told my Oba about an event in which dogs are worshipped. This annual celebration in a small town honors dogs for their contributions to creation. I wish this Oba had explained what creation is, but my Oba already seemed to know, so there was no further discussion about creation. But then as my Oba and the visiting Oba continued their conversation, I heard something so shocking that I hid behind the door. The visiting Oba said to my Oba that this town where the annual celebration is held is perhaps the only town in the whole world without dogs! The village does not allow dogs to live there! I am glad my Oba and his family live in Oshogbo.

I hear many interesting and sometimes surprising things around the palace. One visitor, not an Oba but a priest, came to the palace and announced that he was looking for an animal to be sacrificed to a deity. He told my Oba that it was the year when a dog needed to be sacrificed to the Ogun, the God of Iron. I do not know what 'sacrifice' means. As I listened to this conversation between my Oba and the priest, I wondered whether I would be honored and be selected for sacrifice. But I have not heard mention of this by my Oba — in fact, he seemed anxious to change the subject of their conversation and asked one of his children to take me out into the courtyard to play for the remainder of the priest's visit that day.

Except for the aforementioned visitors, I had a placid life. The Oba, who was a good King, moved on in age, as did I. The Oba's walking pace slowed and became shuffled. So did mine. I had problems holding my head high, as did my Oba. Finally, the time came and my Oba began to prepare for the trip to the Beyond. I lay beside his bed and wondered whether my Oba knew exactly where that trip would take him? I also wondered if he would be taking me along on this journey. And would I know the way if I have to show my Oba where it is he needs to go?

Today, my Oba breathes no more. Elaborate funeral arrangements were made before he departed, and now the funeral has taken over the palace. I am here to observe. Oba lies in a casket, peaceful, and much younger-looking than I have seen him for many years now. He looks happy and I think my Oba must be looking forward to the trip. For several days my Oba's children, my friends Aduke the parrot and Akanni the vulture and I remain beside my Oba while thousands of people pass by the casket. Most of the people are crying, and all are somber.

It is time to close the Oba's casket. The Oba's wives and children have gone into their private rooms. I feel unusually tired. Standing up and taking even a single step seems too difficult and exhausting for my old body. I remain with my friends Aduke and Akanni in the courtyard of the palace. The world is turning dark all around me. It is nightfall, yet a golden ball has appeared in the sky. I hear the beautiful sound of the drums. I look for Akanni and Aduke, but I no longer see them beside me.

The golden orb is becoming larger and larger, closer and closer. Somehow my weary old body is standing, walking towards that bright light. The drums call me and lead the way. And I am not alone. My Oba is next to me. Once again, we are blissfully happy, and the road before us is strewn with ododo flowers. Together, enveloped by the golden light and the rhythm of the drums, we begin our journey to the Great Beyond.

# SEPTEMBER
## The Seven Dog Commandments

IF YOU GIVE ANY THOUGHT and study to the names of the months in our Roman calendar, you will observe a discrepancy between those months with names rooted in a number and their actual place in the calendar year. The months named for a Roman deity or emperor, or named for an obvious attribute found in the time of year the month embodies, are perfectly self-explanatory. But the months — and there are four of them beginning with September — with names rooted in their numeric order in the calendar, appear to have slid out of their proper position. September comes from the Latin *septem*, which means seven. Yet September is the ninth month in the year. October is from *octo*, eight, yet...well, even dogs understand why their masters might refer to the confusions and misnomers of the Roman calendar as a "pet peeve."

This story is about a "pet peeve" of the Dog World — historic and contemporary human mistreatment of canines, socially, culturally, and verbally.

### The World Over

Humans have an explanation for everything, although many times their explanations are wrong. We dogs don't tell them they're wrong, because humans do not tolerate being corrected by a dog. But as this is a story to be read to a dog, I will be truthful.

Just think how confused humans have been throughout history about how to set up a plausible system for social, religious, commercial, or administrative purposes, i.e., everything. They observed the moon, the sun, the seasons, the tide, saw a connection, and came up with what is called a calendar, i.e., days, months, and years. It took hundreds of years for the diverse civilizations and cultures to agree on a calendar that satisfied all of their shared needs. This same calendar is used today almost everywhere in the human world for all civil purposes.

When humans started to assign names to their calendar, real trouble and confusion began; it was difficult to please everybody. It looks today like it was the Romans who won, however. The bickering and jealousies of various Roman gods and emperors resulted in the names of our present calendar months. The first month Janus (January) is named after Janus, the Roman god of gates and doors (with a double-faced head, each looking in opposite directions). Februus (February) was the Etruscan god of the underworld and also the god of purification. Mars (March) was the Roman god of war. Aprilis (April) was not named for a god but is derived from the Latin verb *aperire* and is the month in which the buds begin to open. Maius (May) was the Roman goddess of honor and reverence. Juno (June) was the protector of the Roman state, and as wife of Jupiter, queen of gods. July was named after Julius Caesar, who was both born and assassinated in this month. August honors the first of the Roman emperors, Augustus.

Now we get to the month where the real problem begins: September. Can't the humans count? In all the many languages derived from Latin, it is understood that *septem* means seven. But September is the ninth month in the present-day calendar. And from here on, the name/number problem continues all the way to the end of the year and December.

Of course, we, the dogs, have the explanation. Here is the history in summary form:

September is thus named because it is the month when the Seven Dog Commandments were given to the world. Genghis Canis, Superior Ruler of the whole Dog World, journeyed alone into the mountains where he received from on high the laws by which all dogs and humans shall live. Upon receiving the revelation, Genghis Canis proclaimed the Seven Dog Commandments from the top of Mount Psa. Passed down and spoken dog to dog through the ages, the commandments are herein written in a manner that humans can understand. Although they are given in a numbered sequence, the Seven Dog Commandments were not necessarily imparted to Genghis Canis on Mount Psa in this particular order:

I. *Thou shall not use the word dog in an insulting, derogatory, or offensive manner.*

II. *Thou shall treat dogs with the same — and perhaps more — respect than thou showest your neighbor.*

III. *Thou shall provide dogs the freedom of action inherent in and dictated by our genetic code.*

IV. *Thou shall acknowledge, educate, encourage, and engage dogs in those activities for which we were specifically bred and designed.*

V. *Thou shall not breed dogs in a manner — or experiment with dogs in any way, shape or form — that alters, compromises, or lessens*

*the integrity of our inherent character and
intrinsic nature.*

VI. *Thou shall never use dogs for food under any
circumstances.*

VII. *Thou shall treat dogs as equals, as we shall
do the same for you.*

The Seven Dog Commandments of Genghis Canis were distributed throughout the Dog World and at the time of the ancients seemed to require no further explanations. However, over the centuries, it became clear that not all humans are equally sensitive and intelligent. Therefore, we here provide further clarification and notes about the Seven Dog Commandments as follows:

*Regarding Commandment 1:* Here is some canine food for thought about common but derogatory human uses of the word 'dog.' Humans all too frequently call someone they do not respect a 'son of a bitch!' They even use the phrase as a generic expletive. Because the word 'bitch' is actually the English term for a female dog of any species, this use of the formal term for a female canine is most offensive to our species. Furthermore, we dogs are perplexed as to why a male dog is simply called a 'male' dog, but a female dog is known as a 'bitch.' We dogs would like to suggest that, if humans choose to call our females by a formal term, this term is never used to offend a human, as it then simultaneously offends and insults all dogs and their mothers. Furthermore, when humans refer to an unattractive human female as a 'dog,' you again insult all dogs. We also are perplexed as to why humans call a man a 'lucky dog' but never call a woman a 'lucky bitch.' We respectfully suggest you eliminate that term from your vocabulary. Humans like to insult one another by saying someone is a 'dirty dog.' We dogs suggest you look in the mirror; humans don't always look so clean to us, either. And why would you want to eat a 'hot dog?' And why is one football or basketball team considered the 'underdog?' Why do golfers call a golf course in poor condition a 'dog track?' In general, exactly why would humans insist on calling a contemptible person, and just about anything else considered inferior, substandard, imperfect, even repulsive from a bad speech, to an old car, to an incompetent waitress 'a dog?' You humans wish upon your enemy a 'dog's life,' i.e., a wretched existence. (The implications of this colloquialism have caused the Dog World much consternation. Perhaps a summit about this widely held human supposition is in order?) Humans will suggest that a sick friend is 'dogged' by ill health or unfortunate circumstances. Why are humans not 'dogged' (because many of us dogs are tenacious in the pursuit of a goal, and are persistent in our loyalty to a master) by good fortune and a strong body, thick hair, warm beds and long naps?

We of the Dog World tolerate humans calling us doggie, pooch, barker, bow-wow, honey, or sweetheart. But we much prefer you give us beautiful names befitting our appearance and essence such as Prince, Princess, Sirius, Laika, Bella, Sharik, Arnika von dem Ammersfeld, Asta von der Guglhoeh, Belle, Lily, Precious, Nora, etc. The list of lovely names is endless.

*Regarding Commandment 2:* Ideally, we would all like to have good neighbors. We understand it is not always so. (We bark at and protect you from the unfriendly and not-so-good neighbors.) But we do request that you treat your dog like you would treat good neighbors. Be friendly, helpful, sensitive, responsible, clean, thoughtful, and respectful of boundaries. We share the same space and understand that our habits impose on you, and vice versa. Our number one goal is to please our masters. Even the best of good neighbors will not treat you with the unconditional, twenty-four-hours a-day, seven-days-a-week love that we dogs offer.

*Regarding Commandment 3:* Evolutionary studies have revealed that dogs are probably descended from wolves. We may be distant ancestors of wolves, and we certainly understand and exhibit their 'pack mentality,' but dogs have been what humans call domesticated and tamed. We have been brought into the world of humans to live side by side, together in the same home where we protect, love, and serve our masters. However, there are remnants of the wild side in us. We have genes not found in humans, and this means we need freedom to follow and honor these deeply ingrained traits. For example: Do not tie us to a tree. Doing so inhibits our natural instincts. We become nervous, we get bored; we cannot escape an enemy or defend ourselves. If we are tied up or caged, we cannot exercise and we cannot socialize. We slowly die.

*Regarding Commandment 4:* While we are all members of the genus *Canis* we have branched out to include many different breeds with dozens, if not hundreds, of diverse characteristics and traits.

We are complex and colorful in personality, appearance, and essence. While my sissy pal the Poodle loves to romp, play, and preen, my friend the Beagle must follow every scent, every trail, to its source. Cocker Spaniels are polite and friendly to a fault, and the gentle giants called Saint Bernards will do anything in any weather to save a human life. My neighbor the Border Collie needs to herd something (anything, even other dogs!) or someone, while my old friend with the black spotted tongue, the Chow-chow, focuses exclusively and eternally on the health and safety of her master, the Empress of the House.

I could go on and on about my fellow canines but will stop here. These are only a handful of the hundreds of characteristics and breeds *Canis* includes. We dogs are proud of our diversity and ask that humans defend and honor each breed and its needs and wants.

*Regarding Commandment 5:* If you do not know what dark and terrible things can result from ill-advised experiments, we suggest humans read *Heart of a Dog* by human writer Mikhail Bulgakov. In this story a misguided scientist transplants the testis and the pituitary gland of a human into a dog. The integrity of both species is deeply compromised. Instead of creating something better, the end result of this experiment is a dog with the worst characteristics of both a dog and a human. We strongly recommend dogs be left as dogs, and humans remain humans.

*Regarding Commandment 6:* Remnants of dog bone found in dried human waste unearthed in southwest Texas revealed that nearly 10,000 years ago, man's best friend provided not only protection and companionship, but also an occasional meal! We dogs especially frown upon this practice and ask that humans not tolerate such behavior among even the most primitive of their species in the modern world. It is, in every sense of the word, *inhumane*.

*Regarding Commandment 7:* If you follow each of the previous six commandments, we of the canine world pledge to the human world our unconditional love. We promise to protect you with our lives, to bring happiness to your lives, and to live by your social rules (i.e., become house-trained) to the best of our abilities.

We dogs prefer to live with a loving master. We still enjoy the company of dogs, but we have come to prefer the company of our beloved humans, and our ultimate happiness is to share a lifelong relationship with the people who love us in return.

# OCTOBER
## Sirius the Dog Star

CICADAS ARE INTRIGUING CREATURES. Some wait in the ground and only emerge every thirteen to seventeen years. While most people close their windows when the cicadas start their songs at sunset, for others their sound is like a meditation, soothing and stimulating at the same time. The intense sound cicadas produce can reach a noise level that could cause permanent hearing loss in humans if we were exposed to it at close range for an extended period. People will move away from such extreme sound before it causes permanent damage to their ears. However, a dog tied to a tree may not be able to escape the passionate song of the summer cicadas and may very soon experience hearing loss or even deafness. Cochlear implants provide a potential hearing aid for humans and have been implanted surgically in deaf Dalmatians. However, the cost is prohibitive, and post-implant training is required, making this auditory assistance impractical for dogs. Perhaps one day dogs and their sensitivity to frequencies not heard by humans will assist scientists in their quest to restore hearing to the deaf. This tale tells of just such a scientist and a dog. Unfortunately, although the tragic part of the story is true, the happy ending is all fiction. Dogs and their people can imagine a day when all dog stories have happy endings.

*Abiquiu, New Mexico*

I am a puppy, the cutest little purebred coonhound you've ever seen. The whole family greets me at my new home. Father, mother, son, daughter, are very happy to have me as their puppy. There is laughter, caressing, licking, kissing, doggie-talking, and chasing around in a circle. I am known as Puppy.

The next morning after my wonderful greeting and homecoming in the master's house, I find myself outdoors with a stiff, new collar around my little neck. I am tied to a juniper bush. Yesterday I was able to roam and inspect every inch of the home of my new family, but beginning today my home is in a crate outside. I do have a soft blanket, but surrounding my little crate house there is only the dusty, grassless earth of the yard to sit and sleep on.

Where are the children, where is the master? They all left early in the morning. After a long day sitting alone on the earth by my crate, the children and parents arrive home in their shiny car. I wag and wag my tail, but they leave the car and disappear into their house. They ignore me, but I tell myself they will soon come out and play. Also, I am very hungry. The food bowl is empty, the water bowl is dry. At least the sun which has been hot all day is beginning to set in the west.

I sit waiting. I am so patient. Finally, the door of the house opens. I stand and wag my tail. Oh joy! The mother master approaches me and fills the bowl with food. She pours water in the other bowl. My tail and my bright, happy face tell her how much I appreciate her attention. She pats me quickly, and then she is gone. She disappears into the house. No playing. No talking. No petting. The children do not come outside. It is too hot for them, even in the evening.

This is the first night I am alone and in the dark. Only the stars are my companions. I remain hopeful that in the morning the family will come out and play.

As the sun rises, the whole family comes outside — but not to me. They all climb into the shiny car and leave. I look around.

There is nothing to play with. The soft blanket is my only friend. I chew on it; this is how I can show love, with my little teeth. I walk around the juniper bush that is now my other friend. Alas, my leash is getting shorter and shorter. All of a sudden I cannot move any further. I cannot reach my bowls, my blanket, or my safe place, the crate.

I wait. They will come and help me. They must know I can hardly breathe. It is hot, the sun stands high, the leash is so short. I cannot move into the shade. I am thirsty. Doesn't the family know that I can't just lie around, doing nothing? I'm a puppy! I want to do things for and with my family. I decide to bark so that my family will remember me. I have a loud bark. All coonhounds have a loud bark; we are famous for it. We have a special talent that no other dog has, and I am proud of it: we are treeing dogs. We are hunting dogs, but not like any other hunting dog. In addition to having a keen sense of smell, we are able to track, chase, and corner. We follow an animal that is trying to escape into a tree. We will bark and keep the prey 'treed' until the hunter arrives. We will never bark up the wrong tree!

But my bark has no purpose. I am bored. How thoughtless to leave me alone. I am very good with children. I am affectionate and could dish out love and loyalty if they would just let me. They could talk to me, look into my face. I may not be able to speak, but I communicate in different ways. On this short leash, I cannot even move to tell someone I'm desperately hot and thirsty.

Somebody must have heard my coonhound barks. The neighbor lady climbs over the stone wall and unwinds my leash. Why didn't I think of that? All I had to do was walk around the juniper bush counterclockwise. I wag and lick her hand before she leaves. She smiles and pets me. I wish I were her puppy.

Every day and night are the same. How long can I tolerate this boring existence? Let me think; there must be a way to escape, dig under, climb over? It is summer, hot dog days they call it, but it cools down at night, so soothing for a hot puppy. I am getting ready for a good night's sleep when the stillness is disrupted. There is a busy rustle, a crackle near the bottom of my friend the juniper bush. Finally I have company!

Company, yes. But cuddly, pretty company? No. Beneath the juniper bush ugly brown blobs burrow up and out of the soil. The blobs climb up onto the juniper's branches. When they have reached a high perch they strip off their brown skin. Soon hundreds of bulging eyes stare at me. Over their roof-like bodies are greenish, shiny, semi-transparent wings, which now vibrate. A winged brood, that's what they are. The brood flies seemingly aimlessly around the tree, finally coming to rest. They're not so ugly. I fall asleep happy that I have new friends.

I wake. I do not see the brood. It is quiet all the rest of the night and throughout the next day. I begin to fret. Have they left me, just like my family? The sun is beginning to set, and suddenly there is a hum, changing into what could be called a song. This song is not really beautiful or soothing. It increases in intensity, and my ears begin to ring and ache.

"Please stop," I bark, "you are hurting me." If they are my friends, why do they hurt me?

The painful song is relentless and continues until the dark breaks at dawn. Relief. The song, what I call noise, stops.

This pattern of the brood is repeated for a whole month of days and nights. Fortunately the brood sings its noise only several hours every evening. I bark up at the bush, but these creatures are not impressed, intimidated, or bothered by my coonhound bark. I cannot 'tree' them. The noise continues. Looking closely I see that not all of these creatures make the noise; some just sit, unmoving.

What at first was a totally unacceptable nuisance of a brood living in the juniper bush has become less and less disturbing. Finally their song stops completely. I am puzzled. The creatures' bodies still vibrate, but no sound. And then overnight they are all gone from the juniper.

The world is even quieter than before the brood moved into the juniper. I notice, too, that the birds who sit in the crown of the juniper bush, or that flew by my house, no longer chirp and call. My master's lips move when she feeds me, but I do not hear her. And this makes her face grimace. She frowns as she drops dry food kibbles from a bag into my dish. She speaks and looks irritated as she leaves. I have become accustomed to my solitude. But after the brood leaves, and the birds stop singing, and my master makes words I cannot hear, the solitude becomes loneliness. Why has everything gone silent? Even the rustling of the branches of my juniper has stopped. I am just a puppy, but I have learned that people are the first to leave you, and then nature does the same. If I only had my blanket — I chewed it up long ago. I fall asleep on the dirt and wish I would never wake up again.

Late in the summer something unexpected happens: the kind neighbor woman who often comes over and unwinds my rope from the juniper tree brings a friend to visit. Her friend is very interested

in me, and gives me a treat. He speaks to me — I can see his lips
moving — and looks in my ears. My master comes out of the house
and talks with the neighbor and her friend. And this is when something very surprising happens. My master unhooks my leash from
the stake, and hands it to the man who has been rubbing my ears.

My master then turns and walks back into her house. The man
and the neighbor woman lead me away from my little crate by
the juniper tree, and out onto the dirt road. When we reach a car
parked in the shade beside the neighbor woman's house, the man
unhooks my leash, opens the car door, and directs me to climb into
the rear seat. I am not afraid because this man is so gentle, and
because the kind neighbor woman is smiling. I trust these people.
The man climbs into the front seat and waves good bye to the
neighbor woman. And just like that, we drive away from the sandy
yard, the wooden crate and the juniper tree that has been my home
for all of my life.

I am nervous but I am not sad to leave. I see new houses, big
streets, and very big trees. These trees are much bigger than my
juniper bush. Many houses sit close together, some several stories
high. There are very few yards, but all yards have thick green grass.
I am traveling, and I love it.

We stop at a big gate that opens just for us. We drive up the
hill, and at the end there is a beautiful house with big windows. I
understand that this new man will probably set me down, tie me
up, and leave me. At least there is grass. Instead, he picks me up
and takes me from the car seat and sets me down on the driveway.
I follow him into the house. I have never seen anything like it. One
room after another. Soft floors. Shade and sun both. I am afraid,

but this new man is gentle. We follow this wonderful smell to a room, and the man who I hope is my new master bends down with a bowl of the most delicious food. I have never tasted anything like it. I am then taken to my own bed, the softest bed I have ever dreamed of. I fall asleep. Maybe this is a dream? When I wake up, I expect to be back in my crate. But no, I am still on my soft, warm bed. I deserve this life. I am a good puppy.

One day my new master — yes! He has become my new master — picks me up and takes me out to the car. I am traveling again. We stop at a big house, bigger than my master's, and inside the person behind the counter, a nice young girl, asks for my name. My name is no longer Puppy. I watch my master's lips, and he says, "His name is Sirius."

"How nice," the girl says, "named after the dog star."

I am a star! I am taken into a smaller room. I am feeling a little scared, particularly when a man in a white coat enters the little room. He is a vet. I have never been in a vet's office. But he is gentle, too, and pets me. He looks in my ears and mouth and massages my whole body. A cold gadget is placed on the underside of my body. I am very scared, and my heart starts beating rapidly. But he is gentle, and my master stands right beside me. I watch the vet fill tubes and stab me twice on the back of my neck. It does not really hurt, but it does not feel good, either. Twice is enough. My master and the man in the white coat move their lips, but they don't talk loud enough for me to hear what they are saying. It is alright; I feel secure. I like their body odor.

I get back into the car to go home. But no, we are going somewhere other than home. Master stops the car before an even bigger building, and we go inside. More people in white coats talk with my master and look at me. What are they doing? They are putting wires on my body, particularly near my ears. I let them because they are gentle, they pet me, and because my master is with me. Suddenly from every direction I hear sounds, very high-pitched sounds. My tail wags vigorously. I am excited and happy! More sounds, more tail wagging. My master and the people in white coats applaud and dance around me. They remove the wires and everything goes silent again.

Life is good. Good food, much love, and endless attention. My master is gone during the day, but he makes up for his absence with affection and our walks together. I sleep in the same room as my master, so I am never lonely or afraid in the dark. I don't know what he does when he is gone, but my master has many friends who visit our house and pay attention to me. They sit around the table in the evening and move their lips. I don't know if they have secrets, but they do not talk loud enough for me to hear. Many times they look at me and seem to be talking about me. I see their lips form my name — Sirius. I feel very important when that happens.

One day my master takes me back to the same huge building we visited before. The many humans in white coats gather around me again, and it seems that I am the most important person in the room. They are excited. The person who is the chief puts a collar around my neck with a little box on it. Oh no, I hope they will not tie me to a juniper bush again. I look up at my master. I see in his kind eyes that everything is fine.

They take me into a small room and put more wires on me. My master bends down to me and moves his lips. I have never heard his voice, but now I hear a voice soft and sweet as he moves his lips: "Sirius, can you hear me?"

What is this? I am frightened, but the sound makes me recall something from when I was a small puppy: the human voice! I wag my tail and jump from the chair up onto my master. He laughs and hugs me as I lick his face. The door of the small room opens, and other people crowd into the room and applaud and dance. Are they happy because of me? Yes. I am happy, too, because I can hear again — thanks to the little box on my collar.

In the next days I hear in conversations that my master is a famous scientist. He has developed a box that converts the frequency of human speech to the ultrasound frequency that I can still hear. I learn that the loud, deafening sound produced by the brood of winged creatures — called cicadas — in the juniper bush caused me to lose my hearing in the range humans use to speak. I know from listening to my master that the cicadas are not bad creatures; it was the thoughtless people who tied me to the juniper bush who were bad, although master says they were really not bad, just ignorant.

"Woof!" I say. I am so special! I, as all dogs, can hear frequencies humans cannot hear, and cicadas cannot produce. My master's gadget — the box I wear on my collar — is going to get patented and help many other animals.

My master prepares for a trip. There is an open suit suitcase and clothes and items strewn all over the house. There is also a special bag on wheels with holes in the sides.

"Sirius," master tells me as he packs, "we are traveling."

I have traveled before, but this time is different. We drive to the airport where I am squeezed into a traveling crate — the bag on wheels. I am placed in my traveling bag under a seat beside my master in a strange room with many small windows and many people sitting very close together. There is a loud, scary noise, and we are moving, flying. My master comforts me and reassures me as we travel. I am quiet and do not cause my master any problems. I finally fall asleep. When I wake we are in a place that looks different from any place I have seen. I hear people speak, but I cannot understand a word that they say.

People treat us with great respect. We check into a hotel where I have a special bed, gleaming food bowls, and a wonderful view of the city. The next day we are picked up in a large car, a limousine, and we are taken to a building my master calls a castle where the hallways are lined with mirrors and windows. The surfaces sparkle with gold and silver.

I am the only dog. I like the attention. My master is wearing an unusual suit. He has the aisle seat in the first row of an auditorium. I am sitting next to him. We wait. Many speeches. I don't understand any of them, although I can hear all of them. Then I hear my master's last name. I learned it a long time ago, and it is my last name also. He gets up and he tells me to follow. We take the stairs up to the stage and are greeted by a royal-looking gentleman, a king.

I hear "and the Nobel Prize for medicine goes to…." The man speaks my master's name. There is thunderous applause, a standing ovation, and camera lights flashing. I look at my master with love and pride. He looks at me the same way!

Then hotel, airplane, and we are back home, thank God. This trip has drained my energy. Sleep, sleep, and life goes on as usual. I have a feeling that I have experienced something very special and that I was an important part of it.

I am proud of my master and proud of myself, but I am also sad. Each day I wonder: do I deserve to be so lucky? What can I do to change the fortunes around for all the dogs that grow up like I did in a yard, tied to a juniper bush, lonely, bored, neglected, hungry, thirsty and dirty? Will someone come and rescue them? What about their ears? I wish I had the answer. I will keep listening so if I hear the answer I can pass it along to other dogs with my big coonhound bark.

# NOVEMBER
# The Turkey of Port-au-Prince

THE FIRST MORNING AFTER MY ARRIVAL in Port-au-Prince, I set out from my hotel and was followed by a young man. He was about thirteen years old, and pointed at himself and said "guide." I thanked him for his offer but walked away. In spite of my disinterest, he followed me through the market like my shadow. I was looking at art, paintings in particular. I went through many stalls and shops. Not finding what I was looking for in the marketplace, I finally entered an elegant and expensive gallery. I immediately found several paintings that I liked. As I left the gallery, I was greeted by my shadow. I decided to ask him his name.

"Jean," he answered. "I am artist, have teacher, take you to teacher. Teacher sell painting in gallery." He pointed at the gallery I had just left. "Sell cheaper."

I followed Jean onto a dirt road and up a hill away from the "civilized" tourist part of the city. There was no more vegetation. Chickens crossed the streets from left to right, right to left, aimlessly clucking and pecking. Dogs were curled up asleep or walked and sniffed about the streets looking for food. People stared at me. Finally we reached a hut with a thatched roof and windows with no glass. It was like every other hut on this hillside. There was nothing distinctive about it.

"Teacher live here," Jean said.

Somewhat skeptical, I said: "Your teacher's paintings in the gallery sell for a lot of money. Why does he live here in a shack when he can easily afford a house — a mansion — on the other side of town?"

Jean looked at me and said: "Teacher not only own one hut; teacher own fifty huts!"

This thirteen year old boy taught me a valuable lesson summed up in a favorite proverb: "It is better to be a king among paupers than a pauper among kings."

Every morning the rooster has the audacity to crow and disturb the farm dog's sleep. During the day, the rooster arrogantly struts around the farm with his chest raised disrespectfully calling the dog 'MM.' The dog thinks 'MM' can only stand for 'Mangy Mongrel.' The dog fights back by calling the rooster 'PC,' which stands for 'Pompous Cock.' It is doubtful that the rooster understands his name, as arrogant roosters do not have time to think, in contrast to dogs, even Mangy Mongrels, who have plenty of time to think.

After several days of thinking about the whole situation with the arrogant rooster, MM decides it is time to put a stop to this annoying exhibitionist. The dog decides he will tell PC that, as he is such an elegant rooster, and behaves so gentlemanly, there is a good chance that his master will enter him in a cock fight.

The dog found PC and explained how the master might take him to a cock fight. PC was flattered, of course, and excited. But then MM went on to explain:

"If you are in a cock fight, PC, the best that could happen is that you get killed."

PC stopped strutting and stared at MM in astonishment. MM continued:

"If you're unlucky, you may come out alive, but you will have lost your beauty."

The dog could see that PC was truly worried, at least as worried as time and intelligence allow a rooster to be. The dog offered PC a solution.

"Change your looks and pretend to be a turkey. It is simple. All you need is plenty of dark feathers and a snood and wattle. Most importantly, you have to practice to gobble. Remember, you are a male turkey."

The rooster liked the dog's idea and that day followed MM's instructions to make himself look like a turkey. It was easy to find feathers on the farm from the various chickens. But the rooster was not satisfied with these and started pulling feathers right off the hens. They tried to escape by running and clucking about in different directions, but PC was undeterred and pursued the chickens until they were about to drop from exhaustion. He pulled out feathers and stuck them right into his skin. The pain of all this poking and sticking was overshadowed by the excitement and pride PC felt as he began to resemble a grand turkey.

PC remembered seeing something that looked like a turkey's snood and wattle in the slaughter house that adjoined the farm. It was a disgusting sort of thing to go after, but PC did not notice. After pulling the feathers off the dead rooster's throat and head, he was left with the two attached appendices, held down by feather keels. Little did PC the rooster know but even with these attached to his body he would not be able to attract females: PC could not use the fanlike tail, and change the color of the snood and wattle. He did know, however, how to strut, and PC's boisterous gobble could be heard all over the farm.

The transformation was complete. The dog could see how PC felt even better about himself now. Standing stately like a turkey, PC told MM that he wanted to parade his new look to the people at the other side of town.

"That part of Port-au-Prince is called 'Villa City,'" the dog told the rooster that now looked like a turkey.

PC nodded. "I have never been there, but I have heard that it is ritzy. I think I will blend in nicely."

The dog could see that PC had made up his small mind and so said nothing.

"I will be back when it gets dark," PC said. "I want to sleep in my own coop, at least for a little while longer."

The dog watched PC the rooster-turkey waddle away from the farm and down the hill.

The neighborhood changed gradually from the scruffy hillside of shacks and dirt yards to the paved, clean neighborhoods of large white houses and lush gardens. PC peeked through the fences into these wonderful tropical gardens, partially hiding fabulous mansions. This world was nothing like home back on the farm. PC puffed himself up even larger so that everyone in this fancy neighborhood could see what a fine bird he was.

PC passed one house with a large red, white, and blue flag waving at the top of a tall pole. He stopped to admire the flag and to be admired by whoever lived here. All of a sudden PC felt firm hands clamp around his beautiful body. As he was picked up PC thought: "I knew I would be accepted here. Now that I look different, everyone wants me."

PC was carried into the house, into a large room with big pots steaming over a fire. The people in this house were very busy and very happy to see the beautiful turkey carried in from the garden. PC fluffed up and enjoyed the attention until a sharp pain struck his neck. Everything turned black.

The following day MM awakened late, long after the sun had come up and the other animals on the farm had been fed. The dog stretched and yawned and finally realized that something was askew. PC's loud crowing had not awakened him!

"I hope that rooster turkey is not in trouble," MM thought. "It would be my fault."

MM could hardly admit it, but he was missing that arrogant rooster PC. After eating his breakfast, the dog sat under a tree and stared down the hill through the familiar huts and landscape. No rooster. No turkey. MM decided he would have to go out and look for PC.

The dog descended the hill. When he reached the foot of the hill, the dirt road turned into a paved highway. No more chickens, no more stray dogs, no more shacks. MM did not feel at ease. He did not belong here, but he continued. He had to find PC. He picked up PC's scent and followed it until he reached the mansion with the red, white, and blue flag waving at the top of the flagpole. He stopped. Through the fence he could see a family sitting around a table enjoying a huge feast in the garden. A wonderful smell wafted from the food heaped on the table. MM sniffed the air. It was a delicious scent, but it made him feel uneasy.

At the table the people were talking to one another. MM, who understood everything people said, sat down and listened.

"We are so far away from home," the master of the house said, standing and holding up his glass. "But God is everywhere. Even here on this island, he has blessed us this year with a turkey for Thanksgiving!"

MM was a good thinker, but he wasn't liking what he was thinking. He decided to move on and continue his search for PC.

As he passed the large gates to the house, he looked up and saw a sign on the garden gate: "American Embassy."

MM the dog walked on through the neighborhoods of Villa City, but his heart was not in the search. Finally, as the sun began to set, he headed for home. As he approached the farm and his own little hut, he passed the coop. It was empty. The dog let the thoughts he didn't like to enter his head. PC was gone.

The dog ate his supper and thought how if PC hadn't been so concerned about his appearance, that rooster would still be strutting about. MM could not finish his supper. He had lost his appetite. It was MM who had told PC to pretend he was a turkey!

The dog went to his bed and watched the stars come out. He couldn't eat, he couldn't sleep, and he couldn't blame that arrogant rooster! Worst of all, MM couldn't pretend he didn't miss that Pompous Cock calling him a Mangy Mongrel.

# DECEMBER
## Winter Light

I DON'T REMEMBER WHERE AND HOW I met Fumio, an artist from Japan. Perhaps I first heard about him in my vet's office. His story touched me. When Fumio was thirty-six years old, his dog, Akita, needed expensive treatment for a brain tumor. The surgery had to be done in the United States, so Fumio cashed out his hard-earned pension fund and brought his sick dog to America. Sadly, Fumio's gallant and selfless effort to save his dog's life was unsuccessful. Akita died during surgery. Fumio remained in the United States. He and I became friends, and he shared his story with me. Fumio was raised in the Japanese countryside. His parents were hard-working peasants — simple, honorable people. Fumio had several siblings; he was the oldest. The story that follows is derived from what Fumio told me about his family.

*Hiraizumi, Japan*

Another winter has passed in the town of Hiraizumi. Hiraizumi was once a political and cultural center in the Tohoku (Northeast) province, but today it is a small rural town where only a few of the ornate Buddhist monasteries and temples still remain. It is March and the first healthy green plants are sprouting in the village fields, promising a good year for the farm. The dog, Kawa, bounds about the valley. It is spring and there is a new baby in the family's house. As his name implies, Kawa has unlimited energy, and he flows through each day like the river through the valley.

Kawa has lived with the family on the farm all his life. He has seen the arrival of many babies. Spring has always been the time when the family played out of doors with Kawa, laughed and shed their winter burdens. But this year, even the warm air and longer days have not brought the family outside. The baby coos and cries, but there is no laughter in the kitchen. Kawa sits on the porch step and waits and listens, and soon his spring heart is heavy.

The whole family is in a somber, sad mood because the new baby is another girl, the fifth born to the family. They wanted and needed a boy to help with the farm and to eventually take over.

The spring days come and go, and Kawa spends most of his time alone. It is difficult to enjoy the new green and the warm breezes, but Kawa continues with his customary habits, eating and sleeping, walking over to the temple each day to meet with his friends, and returning to lie on the front step. He is patient, waiting for the day someone in his family comes out of doors to play or walk with their faithful dog, Kawa.

After many days of waiting, Kawa is rewarded. The oldest daughter, Junko, emerges from the house, greets Kawa with a warm hug, and then follows him on his daily walk to the temple. Kawa is delighted to have Junko with him; her name means pure, obedient child, and it perfectly sums up her lovely nature.

When they reach the temple, Junko pats Kawa on the head and then goes in through the gates. Kawa sits down and watches Junko enter the temple. Inside, she finds and talks with Hajime, a young Buddhist monk whom Kawa often visits on his daily walk. Junko tells Hajime the family's troubles. She cries softly about how there are five girls and no boys to inherit and work the farm and take care of them all.

Kawa feels very sad, and wants to go to Junko. But Kawa is a wise dog, and he knows it is not his place.

Hajime the monk is a sage, kind, but also cunning young man. Hajime has not ever been with a woman. He listens to Junko's story and gently comforts her while she cries. Hajime then leaves her and walks off alone into the garden. Kawa watches Hajime contemplate what he has just heard. Finally, Hajime returns to the temple and asks Junko to trust him.

Hajime tells Junko that he can make it possible for her parents to get their wish of a son. Junko stops crying and listens. Kawa listens, too. Hajime explains that for this wish to come true there is a condition. Junko must carry the baby boy, and a Buddhist monk must father the child. Hajime then generously offers to be the monk to father the child that Junko will carry.

Junko is elated and gives herself to Hajime.

Kawa sleeps by the temple gates. A little later in the day, Junko reappears, smiling and happy as she has not been in a very long time. Junko and Kawa walk home in the warm spring sun through the new green fields. Junko is playful and Kawa romps like a puppy in the grass. When they reach the farm and Junko's mother hears the story of her daughter's day at the temple, the mother is very thankful to her daughter. And to the monk, Hajime. Soon mother and daughter begin to sew flowing dresses and baby clothes, talking and laughing together with Kawa sitting at their heels. By summer it seems to Kawa as if both mother and daughter are growing with joy and hope.

Autumn returns and another good harvest is brought in from the fields. Winter is advancing on the farm. Junko is larger than her mother, now, although her mother has become rather round. With the frost all of the family remains indoors except to do their chores. The days are shorter, the nights long and cold. Kawa, who has thick fur and never feels the cold, normally prefers to live outside the house. But just as the days are the shortest and the nights the longest and darkest, Kawa sees a strong, bright light twinkling in the night sky. Kawa has never seen this sparkling light before — he remembers everything he has seen and known — and so Kawa senses that something new is about to happen. Something wonderful.

Kawa feels that the time has come, and one morning decides to move into the house to be close to Junko and her mother. Junko understands that Kawa must watch over her during this wonderful time.

From his place near Junko's bed, Kawa can look out the window and see the bright, new star twinkling in the night sky. Outside, the night is very long and very cold, but the dark is lit by the new star in the sky. It is the same in the house. A new baby is born to the family. It is a healthy boy, and he lights up the house just as the new star lights up the night. Junko's father is called in, and Kawa sees something he has not seen in a very long time: a big smile brightens up the father's face.

"A savior is born," the father says. Kawa looks about at the family. Everyone is happy, beaming like it is the first day of spring. December will never be dark again.

IsOLDE KoNA-DovaLE makes her home in a solar adobe house on the high desert of northern New Mexico. A native of Oberammergau, Germany, she travels the world with her beloved Dachshund, Arnica. Isolde, a research scientist, holds a PhD, and has published academic studies on the ear. Formally trained in ballroom dancing, Isolde teaches Argentine tango in the United States and journeys to Buenos Aires to dance with the tango masters. *Tales for Asti: Twelve Stories to Read to Your Dog* is Isolde's first book of fiction. It is the favorite book of her companion Arnica, who heartily recommends *Tales for Asti* to dogs and their friends and families the world over.

www.ingramcontent.com/pod-product-compliance
Lightning Source LLC
Chambersburg PA
CBHW072016170626
46813CB00005B/2166